PENGUIN BOOKS

IN COLD DOMAIN

Anne Fine was born in Leicester and now lives in County Durham. For many years a distinguished writer of children's books, her novel for older children, *Goggle Eyes*, was awarded the Carnegie Medal and the *Guardian* Children's Fiction Award and was filmed by the BBC. *Flour Babies* also won the Carnegie Medal and the Whitbread Children's Novel Award. Her book *Madame Doubtfire* was filmed as the highly successful *Mrs Doubtfire*, released in 1994.

Her first adult novel, *The Killjoy* (Penguin, 1994), was originally published to great acclaim in 1986. In 1990 she followed this success with *Taking the Devil's Advice*, which is also published by Penguin. Her work has been translated into over twenty languages.

In Cold Domain

ANNE FINE

PENGUIN BOOKS

PENGUIN BOOKS

Published by the Penguin Group
Penguin Books Ltd, 27 Wrights Lane, London W8 5TZ, England
Penguin Books USA Inc., 375 Hudson Street, New York, New York 10014, USA
Penguin Books Australia Ltd, Ringwood, Victoria, Australia
Penguin Books Canada Ltd, 10 Alcorn Avenue, Toronto, Ontario, Canada M4V 3B2
Penguin Books (NZ) Ltd, 182–190 Wairau Road, Auckland 10, New Zealand

Penguin Books Ltd, Registered Offices: Harmondsworth, Middlesex, England

First published by Viking 1994
Published in Penguin Books 1995
3 5 7 9 10 8 6 4 2

Printed in England by Clays Ltd, St Ives plc

I

I

Peas in a pod

'We'll arrive early, and then we can admire your mother's deforestation project.'

As he spoke, Caspar was watching the traffic slew into the roundabout, so William didn't have to smile. At any other time, he would have found the remark amusing. One of the reasons he had stayed with Caspar was that, on bad days, Caspar could send truth winging into his black thoughts clad in the frippery of joke, and light up everything. But last night's dream was still a bit too real. William could still taste the chill air and feel the cold on his skin as, in the magical blue winter half-light, he pushed open the gates of Cold Domain, and saw the garden as it used to be.

Now Caspar was swinging the huge car around the last corner.

'What will it be this time, do you reckon? Place your bets.'

William dreaded to think. On the last visit, it had been the rockery. 'Stupid thing. Impossible to weed, and people kept tripping over it.' The time before, it had been the turn of the vine. 'No, it was dead, dear. Quite dead.'

'But only last summer you were complaining that it was forcing its way up between the panes.'

Her mouth had gone tight as a cat's arse.

'No, dear. You've got it all wrong. That vine's been dead for years.'

Caspar dropped a hand on his knee.

'Brace up.'

And he did try. Raising his head, he took a deep breath as they drove through the gates. Too deep a breath, for Caspar turned to look at him suspiciously.

'You're crying already!'

'No, I'm not.'

Credit where it was due, Caspar was a superb driver. Within a second he was in reverse, easing the car back out on to the narrow lane.

'Do you suppose she spotted us?'

'I think it's safe until you're past the lilac.'

'Lilac?'

Silly. The lilac had gone years ago.

'Oh, God! Give me a minute and I'll get a grip.'

'No hurry.'

Caspar got out of the car and lit a cigarette, then leaned on the bonnet and watched William steadily through the glass as he snivelled and mopped, mopped and snivelled. What Caspar couldn't understand was why William ever wanted to come on these god-awful trips in the first place. It was a topic he had raised only a few nights before when William started up the dread litany: 'I really ought to go and see her. It's been *months*.' Caspar had rolled away irritably in the bed. 'Why? If she wants to see you, why can't she make the effort to come to you?'

'What, here?'

'Why not?'

Why not, indeed? There was, after all, a perfectly comfortable spare room. The walls weren't paper thin. And there was nothing odd about Caspar's flat: nothing chichi, no leathers or feathers, no strange friends trolling in and out at even stranger hours.

4

'She's quite all right without you, anyway. She has Barbara.'

'Well, that's the point, isn't it? It's not really fair on Barbara.'

'Barbara doesn't mind. And if she did, she could always ask you to take a turn. Or ask Tory. Or Gillyflower.'

'Oh, I see. Suddenly you're not just an expert on everything else in the world. You're also an expert on my family!'

And then had come the row, and the cold truce. And only after both of those had been spun out as long as William dared risk, and Caspar could stand, had come the hot repentant fuck, and then the glorious peace. No doubt about it, in the ways and wiles of emotional tyranny, William took after his mother. Peas in a pod. But Caspar didn't have to keep leaning hard against the glossy warm flank of his Rover to stifle his lust for Mrs Collett. Now, shifting uncomfortably, he looked hopefully through the windscreen at William, only to cop a fearsome glower in return. And maybe it was the wrong moment. But Caspar couldn't help it; he was born that way. Things that turned others off – tears, running noses, hiccups, hacking coughs – always turned Caspar on more.

He tried one last time.

'Want to drive back as far as the common?'

William pretended that he hadn't heard. Sliding down further in the seat, he laid his head back. Shoulders down. Breathe out slowly. Take your time.

The footsteps tap-tapping to the side of the car took both of them entirely by surprise. She must have fairly streaked along the drive, unless she'd been lurking behind one of the very few bushes still reprieved in what used to be the shrubbery.

'Hiding, dear?'

'Not at all.' William was bolt upright in a shot. 'Caspar is trying to pretend he's stopped smoking, so he thought he'd have one last drag out here, before he runs into Barbara.'

Safe out of Mrs Collett's line of sight, Caspar shook his head in astonishment. He never failed to be amazed how quickly William's mind worked in the presence of his mother.

'You're looking pale, dear.'

'No, I'm not.'

'You should have washed your face.'

Was she going to push her luck? Flash Caspar one of her conspiratorially coquettish smiles, and try to force him into joining her – 'Shouldn't he, Caspar?' – in infantilizing her son even further? Catching the small move that showed William almost raising his hand to rub obediently at the streaks left by his tears, Caspar yearned to stretch across, snatch Mrs Collett by her inflexible silver perm, and shake her hard. Or shake William. Why did he and his sisters put up with it? Either their mother was mad, or she was intolerable. If she was mad, how could she go on having such a dire effect on them? William was nearly thirty, for God's sake. And Barbara was getting on for ten years older. Neither lived in a shoe cupboard. They had friends, and jobs. How could this steely relict from their childhood still reduce one of them to gibbering down the telephone, and the other to regular bouts of weeping? Why couldn't they just do as he and most of his patients did with their own sad, bad, mad, dreary parents: either learn to cope, or bale out?

Still, best to come to the rescue before there was another flood of tears.

''Morning, Mrs Collett.'

Rude woman, just pretending he wasn't there until it suited her.

'Good morning, Caspar.'

'Lovely day. I expect you've been busy in the garden.'

It worked, anyway. Now she was drawing her sclerotic coiffure back through the window, letting William breathe.

'Indeed, yes. I've been round these bushes. They're looking nice and tidy now, aren't they?'

Barren was what they were looking. Practically *bare*. There was almost nothing left of them. And surely you weren't supposed to be able to see all the way to the scullery window from here? Caspar couldn't claim to know the garden all that well, but surely there used to be some kind of tree or bush beside that –

'Mother! Where's the philadelphus? Have you chopped it down?'

'I had to get rid of it, dear. It was frozen.'

'Frozen?'

'In that cold snap. I really did hope it would come round again, remembering how much your father loved it. But I'm afraid it wasn't strong enough.'

'You can barely have given it a chance! That cold snap was only a few weeks ago!'

On cue, the lips tightened.

'Have you come all this way to criticize?'

Caspar was just about to step in again when he noticed Barbara rounding the curve in the drive. Already she was hurling her cigarette aside and waddling faster. Oh, good old Barbara! Let her roll up and deploy her hard-won professional skills. Break it up before it got started.

'Our William? Criticizing? Surely not!'

'William was just telling me off for getting rid of the philadelphus, dear. As if it hadn't almost broken my heart. It was your father's favourite, you know. Each year when it blossomed he'd say to me, "That's it, then, Lilith. Summer's finally arrived."'

'He wouldn't have got round to saying it yet this year, then, would he?' William countered sullenly.

But Mrs Collett had had enough. Her tone snapped the conversation off like yet another unruly root in what was left of her shrubbery.

'Well, it's gone now, so there's no point in discussing it.'

Turning sharply, she set off at a clip towards the house, affecting not to care whether or not anyone followed her. Sighing, Caspar pushed himself off the side of his car, and skirted the open door to slide back in the driving seat. He switched on the engine, and let it idle until William and Barbara had chased their mother far enough round the curve in the drive to be able to step sideways on to the tennis court, out of his way. Then he cruised past them, to draw up underneath one of the few trees in the garden that might survive Mrs Collett's arboricultural depredations, partly by virtue of its sheer size, and partly because it helped to prop up the wall between Cold Domain and the hotel next door. And it was at this wall that Caspar glanced with such longing as he swung the car door shut. Behind it, the wrought-iron tables would still be standing on the lawn, under their drooping umbrellas. The little secret paths would still lead between the rhododendrons to the potting shed. But would he and William manage to

8

slip away for five minutes, for old times' sake? Doubtful. Very doubtful. And even as Caspar yearned for one brief glorious flashback to all the blinding excitement of that first afternoon, William's last graceless remark as they were leaving the flat rang in his ears. 'You don't *have* to chum me. I could always take the train.'

Sighing again, he followed all of them around the corner and saw once more, as he saw first time, last time, every time between, just what it was about Cold Domain that drew William over and over. The sloping lawn now spread down towards the trees unhindered by the rockery she'd uprooted. The old stone tank in which the goldfish lazily used to cruise had been scrubbed free of moss with neat household bleach. Even the rose trellis walk seemed to have disappeared since the last visit. But still the garden's beauty was indestructible. The less there was, the more lovely what remained appeared. Small wonder William woke, drenched with sweat, and clutched him in the night. 'I had the dream again, Caspar. But it isn't a dream, you know. I really do go back there. Back in time. I really was in Cold Domain the way it used to be.'

And there you have it, thought Caspar. You could grow up, as he had, with nothing but the view of next door's slimy brick wall to distract you from your studies. Or your childhood could be spent in some place as magical as this, and you could spend the rest of your days and nights, as William spent his, haunted by dread and loss. And, by God, the woman was getting worse. As Caspar set foot on the wide flagged steps leading up to the house, he heard Mrs Collett's idea of a conciliatory remark drifting back towards him.

'I've had that achillea up, too. Messy, smelly stuff.'

Sighing for the third and last time, Caspar followed them indoors.

2

'Funny friends, dear'

Caspar didn't think of himself as a sadist. Nonetheless, it was with as much amusement as interest that he settled back in his chair to watch the ritual humiliation of poor Barbara.

'No, really, dear. I'd love to see your photographs. We all would.'

Gilly, as usual, said nothing. But William, true to form, attempted to rescue his sister.

'Oh, *no*, Mother. Don't make her bring out her photos. We've seen them already.'

'*I* haven't.' The tone was perfect for its purposes. Light, with a touch of hostess. So Barbara trailed off to fetch her photographs, only to endure the indignity of Mrs Collett's relentless inattention. 'Is that an *insect* crawling on the carpet, dear? Oh, no. Sorry. It's just a thread from Gilly-flower's skirt.' 'Is anyone longing for more coffee? Just sing out if you are.'

Several times, Barbara attempted to gather up the photos.

'Look, this is silly. William and Gilly have seen them anyway. I'll show them to you later.'

'No, dear. It's all right. We're nearly finished now.'

Even soft Barbara had been stung enough by this to point out the obvious fact.

'You don't *have* to look at them.'

'I *want* to see them, dear. I'm *interested*. Look, here's

another of all your poor souls lined up in their wheelchairs. Was it somebody's birthday?'

Patiently, Barbara pointed out the Princess Royal.

'She hasn't bothered to dress up much for you, has she?'

William stuck up for his sister.

'Even princesses have to wear their worst clothes somewhere,' he said. 'Best to do it where they might get the folds caught in the spokes of a wheelchair.'

Caspar joined in for the hell of it.

'Or people might throw up on their shoes.'

'Or bump into them, having fits.'

Lowering her head to hide her most unprofessional smile at this little rally of support, Barbara swept up the last of the photos of the people in her unit. The other packet she had laid aside slipped off her knee on to the rug, and Mrs Collett dived to snatch it up.

'And these, dear?'

Barbara reached out for them.

'You don't want to be bothered with those. They're awful. They're just some of my friends at a party.'

'I'd like to see your friends. I'm always interested in my children's friends.'

Caspar's eye went instantly to William. But he was making the usual effort to appear relaxed, and wouldn't meet his gaze. Gilly was covertly watching her brother though, Caspar noticed. And Barbara tried, again, to take back the photos of her friends.

'Really, Mother. That's it. Show's over.'

Mrs Collett gripped the envelope more tightly.

'Let me just take a peep.'

'It's not worth it. They're terrible photos. And you don't know any of the people.'

Mistake, thought Caspar.

'I don't know any of your patients either, dear. But I was interested in them.'

Defeated, Barbara shifted on to her great beefy knees beside her mother's chair.

'Well, this is Howard. He's really our finance officer, but he's actually a lot more help than some of the trained staff. That's Ellie. You've heard me talk of her, of course. These are Bunster and Dido. They're helpers. That's Phil. You saw a lot of him in the last set –'

She gave up. Her mother was shuffling through the photos with such ferret speed it made no sense at all to go on naming names at her.

'And who are these?'

Mrs Collett held up the photo.

'Just friends. Just some friends.'

'Funny friends, dear.'

Unbelievable. The woman was looking around for encouragement. She was holding up a photo of four men, two pairs arm in arm, clearly surprised in a social quartet at a party, then pushed in line and made to smile for Barbara's camera. If the one open shirt hadn't flashed its message at you, the extra rings surely would. William's face was a perfect mask now. And Gilly appeared to have taken the precaution of going temporarily deaf and blind.

Caspar waited. So did Barbara. And Mrs Collett gave a little laugh.

'Really, dear! I think your friends look like a shower of poofs.'

Proud of the phrase, she repeated it.

'A shower of poofs!'

The strained silence lasted only till Tory's tinny little French garden shed on wheels put-putted round the curve in the drive and drew to a halt outside. But even after the rest had risen to go and greet her, Caspar sat tight, wondering what sort of woman, what sort of power, could keep four grown people from reminding her that her own son was a faggot, and right beside him was a funny friend.

3

Miguel-Angel Gippini Algarón Lopez de Rego

Barbara was squatting on the rug, pleased for once to be the centre of attention.

'Do sit in a chair, dear,' Mrs Collett whispered, a little too loudly. 'You look like a beached whale.'

Barbara blushed, but she sat tight.

'I'm glad we're all here at last,' she said mysteriously.

'Not all of us,' Mrs Collett reminded her. 'George isn't here. Neither is Angus.'

'You can't count Angus,' Gillyflower defended her absent spouse. 'He can't go anywhere, the way the shifts are now at Horridge's.'

'If I'd brought George, I'd have had to have brought the twins,' said Tory. She said no more than that, but even Caspar, who hadn't met the twins, felt that he understood.

'The point is,' Barbara said, 'I have some news.'

She's going to get married, thought Caspar.

'News?'

'What do you mean, "news"?'

'Spit it out, Barbara.'

'I'm going to get married!'

There was silence. Were they all suddenly taken up with the image of Barbara in bed with a man? Certainly the chorus, when it came, was just those few seconds too tardy for comfort.

'That's marvellous, Barbara!'

'Are you really?'

'Who's the lucky fellow?'

'Well, dear. This *is* a surprise.'

Mrs Collett's eyes dropped to a tiny mark on the chair arm, and she began scrabbling with a fingernail. First things first. It was left to the others to start up the obligatory barrage of questioning, since it was clear to them all that this was neither the time nor the place for any doubts or anxiety.

'So who is it, Barbara? Is it Phil?'

'Is it your new finance man? What's his name? Howard?'

Barbara was laughing.

'No, it isn't Howard. Or Phil.'

'Oh, come on, Barbara. Tell, or we'll thump you. What's his name?'

'His name is −' She rocked on the carpet, taking a giant breath. '− Miguel-Angel Gippini Algarón Lopez de Rego.'

She'd clearly been practising, thought Caspar. The faintly canine g, the lisping z, the rolling r − all sounded perfect.

'My God! What a mouthful!'

'What a name, Barbara! Honestly!'

And from the armchair came, 'Oh, *foreign*, is he?' as if in this lay the explanation for which Mrs Collett had been sitting waiting. Only a foreigner would have poor enough judgement, be lonely or warped or − ' oh, *say* it − simply sex-crazed enough to want to marry the giant, hopeless tub of lard she suffered for a daughter.

'He's terribly nice,' said Barbara. 'You'll like him. You all will.'

'I'm sure we will,' Mrs Collett told her. 'It's just . . .'

Her words drifted off. Over her face came that same glazed look Caspar had seen on his own mother's face (before he stopped visiting), and on William's whenever some imagined wrong or slight was being industriously blown up to cannonball size. It spoke of disappointments patiently endured, humiliations hard swallowed. It was probably, thought Caspar, the justified look of motherhood worldwide the day the letter comes announcing the wedding (over), the spouse (unmet). But Mrs Collett had clearly decided to try it on for size anyhow.

'It's just I think it would have been a bit nicer if –'

She broke off, and, tossing her head, gave one of her tragic brave smiles. 'Oh, never mind. We must be happy today. Happy for Barbara. It's lovely for you, dear. Now tell us everything. What does he do? Where did you meet him? And where are you planning to get married?'

It can't have escaped anyone's notice that Barbara chose to answer the last question first.

'Where? Well, here, of course.'

'*Here*, dear?' Mrs Collett gave a little laugh, as if the idea was ridiculous. 'Oh, I don't think so, dear. Not here.'

Barbara looked crushed.

'But –'

Firmly, Mrs Collett repeated herself. 'No. Not here, dear. I don't think so.'

With Barbara stunned into silence, and neither of her sisters sticking up for her, William felt obliged to tackle their mother himself.

'Why not? This is Barbara's home, after all.'

'William!' Another little laugh. 'Barbara hasn't lived here for ages. Have you, dear? Not for *years*.'

Barbara lifted her face, but couldn't speak. She felt

betrayed, as if, deftly, years of daughterly concern were being brushed aside. The calls from drab corridors in which she'd shivered, waiting for her chance at the one phone. The regular visits. 'I'm coming your way on Saturday. Shall I pop in?' The dozens of small thoughtfulnesses: cards on her mother's birthday, flowers on anniversaries, and special care around the weeks that would forever be associated with Hector's last horrid illness. She knew she hadn't always got it right. Indeed, the trail of tearful late-night telephone calls to her brother were testimony to her most obvious failures: the lovingly selected cardigans barely unwrapped, and certainly never worn; the carefully chosen frozen meals for two shoved hastily out of sight in the freezer – 'Perhaps I'll feel more like biryani another day'; even the cheerful little stories of life at the unit suddenly undermined by her mother's discreet peck at the watch face tucked underneath her sleeve. But still, through everything, she had assumed one simple fact: that Cold Domain was home. Naturally most of her clothes were now stuffed in the cupboard in the room that came with her job at the unit. All her tapes and cassettes were there, too, under her bed, along with her spare downie, the bathroom scales she had been given on her twenty-first, and all her shoes and boots. But home is surely where the heart is, and her heart was still in the room at the end of the landing, with its sprigged yellow curtains and the padded velvet seat in the bay window out of which you only had to lean to touch the blossom on –

No! Her heart was somewhere else now. For ever, for certain, (and soon officially), her heart lay with Miguel-Angel Gippini Algarón Lopez de Rego.

'It's quite all right,' she assured William, though he

could see her lip was trembling. 'I don't mind. It's who you marry that counts, not where you do it. And there's a perfectly nice reception room attached to our long-stay unit.'

'Nothing attached to your unit could be nice,' William declared. 'That entire building is an absolute eyesore.'

Ignoring Gilly's obvious nervousness, and Tory's warning frown, he looked meaningfully at his mother. But Mrs Collett chose to pretend that the inadequacies of the Fellaham hospital architects bore no relevance whatsoever to the matter in hand, and were simply of interest in their own right.

'Your father always said that if the people who designed these places were forced to live in them, even for a week –'

William interrupted.

'She *can't* get married at her unit. She just can't. Admit it. It would be impossible. For one thing, she'd have to invite the whole lot of them. Imagine a wedding with all Barbara's protégés! It wouldn't be a ceremony. It would be a disaster. She wouldn't be able to pick her way to the front for wheelchairs, or make herself heard over all the noise.'

He should have stopped right there. But, being William, he had to let the dramatics of the occasion run away with him.

'The whole idea's ludicrous,' he announced. 'I'm sorry, Mother, but it's out of the question.'

Her eyes went marble hard. Still, Caspar thought, if everyone kept up the silence long enough, they might funnel her into enough of a spasm of embarrassment (if not guilt) to scoop back a victory. But Barbara blew it, bursting into tears. It was extraordinary. The first drops spurted from her eyes with such force that they missed her cheeks completely, and fell on the carpet.

19

'It isn't fair!' she wailed. 'I want to get married *here*.' Like a child, she dashed the greasy sheets of tears sideways with her palms. 'I *always* wanted to get married here. Why *can't* I? Gilly did. And Tory would have, too, if she and George had had a proper wedding. It isn't my fault that I've had to wait so long to find the right person. Gillyflower was lucky. She married at *eighteen*. I've had to wait and wait. And now, when I've finally found Miguel-Angel, you're telling me it's too *late*!'

The appalled look on Mrs Collett's face soured to disgust as Barbara's wails degenerated into half-baked snivelling. Even before Barbara came out with her last horribly blubbered 'It isn't *fair*!', the door had clicked shut behind them.

Mrs Collett had fled.

4
Toc-toc-toc-THUD

'Now look what you've done,' scolded Tory. 'You've upset her.' Hastily she swept her eyes round the group. 'Who's going to go after her?'

Caspar was horrified. There was poor Barbara, bawling her eyes out on the rug, and Tory was fussing about her mother.

'Quick! Who's going? Shall I?'

'You're best at it,' said Gillyflower.

'It's no use my going,' William declared in what Caspar took to be, on home ground, his best shot at rebellious defiance. 'I think she's being really mean.'

Barbara lifted her tear-sodden face.

'Do you?' she implored him. 'Do you *really*?'

Before William could answer, Tory was once again upbraiding her sister.

'Don't be ridiculous, Barbara. Only a minute ago you were saying it's not *where* you marry that matters, but *who*.'

'And no one yet knows anything about him,' remarked Caspar.

He'd thought it might snap them out of it. He was disgusted. They were behaving like horrible, craven infants. He'd never come down here again. Next time, he'd take William at his graceless word, and let him catch the train. But instead of pulling themselves together and trying to comfort their sobbing sister by asking her – better late than never – a few basic questions about her future spouse, Tory and Gillyflower completely ignored what he said.

'You'd better hurry, Tory, if you're going.'

'It might be better if there's two of us . . .'

'Do you think so?' Snatching up her woolly, Gilly hurried to the door after her sister, leaving William and Caspar in charge of the weeping Barbara.

'Come on, Babs,' William said forcefully. 'Buck up. It's not the end of the world.'

Caspar felt like walking out. And not because he was unnerved by Barbara's tears. No one in his profession could afford to be rattled by the sights and sounds of anguish. He'd stood at enough bedsides where women drowned in noisy grief. He'd slid boxes of tissues across his desk towards young girls to whom he'd had to break the news that there would never, no, I'm afraid, *never* be any chance of having a baby. A gynaecologist, like an oncologist, saw the chips falling the worst way more often than most. He'd seen the depths of female misery. A dozen times a week, he scribbled the letters A.H. (Abandon Hope) on the top of a full set of case notes, and called the pair in for his bracing little speech. What was a wedding, here or anywhere, compared with that? Nothing. But still, why hadn't a single one of them dropped to their knees on the rug beside their unhappy sister and cuddled her, coaxed her, comforted her in her distress? What was wrong with the whole bloody family?

He couldn't stand any more. Leaving the room, he thundered upstairs to the lavatory, and tugged the laundry box closer to the window. He pulled out his cigarettes. Oh, what an awful house! He thought his own family was frightful, but really, they wouldn't be in the running here. This place was truly *grim*.

A steady *toc-toc-toc* outside the window drew his attention back. He stared out. Miles away down the garden he could see a small figure dementedly hacking with a hoe at the creepers round the base of the potting shed. Behind her stood Tory and Gillyflower, no doubt imploring, persuading, trying to soothe. *Toc-toc-toc-toc*. She'd have the shed down if she wasn't careful. Some of these old wooden structures were held up by the greenery around them. So this was how the garden was despoiled. Mrs Collett's demonic practices, slash and burn, stemmed from her battles with her children. Small wonder William woke in cold sweats, and Barbara stuffed her fat face, and Tory and Gillyflower ranked their sister's extraordinary good news beneath an old woman's irritation. The whole survival of the garden they loved lay in their trust. Put one foot wrong and –

Toc-toc-toc-toc-toc!

Why didn't one of them snatch the hoe out of her hand? If they waited for Mrs Collett to calm down of her own accord, there'd be nowhere to store the mower or hang the spade. Should he go down and help? His arrival on the scene might distract her. Or it might not. He'd seen enough of William in his tempers to guess there was little or nothing to be done.

Caspar stubbed out his cigarette against the pitted stone of the outer sill, and flicked the butt into the flowerbed beneath. There weren't many flowers in it – not enough to hide his cigarette end, anyway. He could see it gleaming up at him. Bloody place! No wonder George and Angus never came. He'd never met either of them.

Tory and Gillyflower dutifully rolled out excuses for them time after time. But they themselves stayed at home. And they were right. The price of love couldn't be this high. He wouldn't come again.

Restored, Caspar pulled down the window. *Toc-toc-toc-THUD*.

5

'... and special portable toilets for the handicapped'

On the way down, Caspar ran into Barbara who was sitting on the bend in the stairs, juggling a cigarette, an ashtray and a sodden ball of tissue. Caspar lowered himself beside her.

'Here,' he said, fishing in his pocket. 'Have a hanky.'

'Oh, thank you, Caspar.' Barbara sniffled and blew, dropping ash in the hanky as she folded it over to blow again.

Caspar patted her on the nearest mammoth knee.

'I'll be all right in a minute,' she tried to assure him. 'I can't think why I'm so upset.'

'Why shouldn't you be upset?' said Caspar. 'For no reason I can fathom, your mother's just been unforgivably mean to you.'

She lifted her swollen, blotchy face.

'No, you really can't blame her,' Barbara said. 'She's embarrassed.'

Caspar could scarcely believe his ears. It must have showed, because Barbara repeated herself.

'No, you can't, Caspar. After all, I am horribly fat. And I'm clumsy. And I'm far too old to be a bride.'

'Barbara —'

In full flow, she cut him off.

'And Mother knows the unit's been my life. Even if I leave out everyone I can, still half my guests will be strange-looking people in wheelchairs. And they'll all have to have helpers. And all the helpers wear Crimplene and smoke all the time. They'd probably smoke right through the service if somebody didn't stop them. And there would have to be signs hung on the gate for the drivers, and ramps laid all over, and special portable toilets for the handicapped. And Mother's just terribly embarrassed. She hates things like that. You can't blame her.'

Caspar was silent. He couldn't blame Mrs Collett, no. It did all sound rather horrible.

Yes, he could. He could blame Mrs Collett. Here was Miguel-Angel Gippini Whatever de Rego, after all, presumably prepared to have his own wedding turned into a beargarden for love of Barbara. Here was William, apparently ready to hire a suit and pick his way between the ranks of palsied well-wishers and their fidgeting helpers, to give his sister away. And even he, selfish and unsociable Caspar, would be prepared to have his floors scuffed and his doorframes chipped by champagne-steered wheelchairs if any good friend of his asked him.

'Your mother's a selfish old bat.'

Barbara shredded the tissue ball into soggy strips.

Caspar persisted.

'Frankly, I don't know how you can even have *wanted* to hold your wedding party here.'

'I always dreamed —'

'Yes?'

She took a breath, and tried again.

'You can't imagine what it's like, Caspar. It's as if you're not truly yourself when you're not here. Sometimes I lie in bed in that dingy little room in Fellaham, and nothing round me seems real. I think myself back here, and I can feel myself coming alive again. Oh, yes! I think. It was summer. Always summer. I can feel the warmth of the stone paths under my bare feet. I go dizzy from the smell of sweet peas. And then, quite suddenly, I've moved into one of those still, silent, end-of-summer days when even the air around seems to be waiting. Just waiting. And, sure enough, after a bit I'm in glorious leaf-kicking October. I can hear apples falling beside me. I actually hear the thuds as they land in the grass. Autumn! I think. Yes! Autumn went on for ever. It was the best time. You could step out in the morning and every bush was coated in brilliant, glittering spiders' webs, and there were patches of mist you could stir with your legs as you walked along. Autumn was wonderful. And then you remember winter. Black twigs against cold blue. Pink and silver skies. Glistening frost –'

There were tears rolling down her cheeks again. She wasn't William, so Caspar couldn't reach out and catch them, and lick them off his finger. Instead, he watched.

'If the wedding is anywhere else,' said Barbara, 'I'll only feel half married. Half of my heart is in that garden. Don't you see?'

'I see,' said Caspar, though he didn't really, and he was saying it to William anyhow.

6

'*That's how they do it in Spain*'

'Poor Barbara.' William's eyes lit with pity as he listened. 'Poor, poor Barbara.'

'Nonsense,' snapped Caspar. 'The four seasons don't just happen in your garden. What your sister needs is to get out of that horrible hospital unit, and join a rambling club.'

He caught William's arm, and twisted it behind his back firmly, to the edge of pain.

'We're slipping away next door now,' he told him. 'Just for five minutes. For a little drink.'

'We ca—'

'Yes, we *can*.'

But they couldn't, for Tory was coming round the corner in search of them. Caspar dropped William's arm as though it had scorched him, then stood resenting his own cowardice while Tory asked, 'How's Barbara? Is she all right now?'

'Caspar's just sent her off to wash her face.'

In unconscious imitation of one of her mother's habits, Tory scratched at a non-existent stain on her sleeve. 'Gilly was just saying what a pity it is Barbara can't get married from their house.'

'Can't she?'

'Not really. Not with Angus working all hours.'

'What about yours?'

Tory couldn't dismiss the idea quickly enough.

'Oh, no. She wouldn't want to do it from ours. You see, George is about to start on the extension.'

'That's it, then,' said Caspar. 'Barbara's wedding is off.'

Immune to sarcasm, Tory stared at him. But William's conscience was pricked.

'Caspar! What about us? Why can't she do it from our place? It's big enough, for heaven's sake. We could even manage a few wheelchairs.'

He didn't forget to flash one of his glorious, crinkly smiles, and Caspar, in any case, felt that he'd brought the roof down on himself. Pity for Barbara fought with revulsion at the idea of any such social occasion. But surely he and William wouldn't be expected to organize anything themselves. They'd just be offering the use of the flat. There'd be inconvenience, of course. And loss of privacy. And no doubt a tremendous waste of time: endless phone calls, waiting in for deliveries, that sort of thing. But no real *responsibility*. It wouldn't kill them.

'Fine,' he said. 'Fine by me. So long as Barbara and this Miguel chap —'

'Miguel-*Angel*.'

The interruption came from Barbara, who had appeared again at the top of the stairs.

'Excuse me?'

'It isn't just Miguel.' Her voice was high and tight, as if her little weep had made no difference to the state of her nerves. 'You have to say Miguel-Angel. It's all one name. You're not supposed to split it up. That's how they do it in Spain.'

His generous offer left dangling, unacknowledged, in the air, Caspar was reduced to a mutter of apology.

Tory stepped in.

'Barbara, you ought to be thanking Caspar, not telling him off. It's very nice of him to say you can get married from his flat.'

'But I don't *want* to get married in London!'

Oh, God! thought Caspar. Is she off again? And clearly Tory thought the same. 'Suit yourself,' she said tartly, and turned, exasperated, on her heel. 'I have to get back to Mother. She'll be getting upset.'

'Upset?' said Caspar. 'Your mother?'

But Tory had already disappeared round the corner.

William laid a hand on Barbara's arm.

'Come on, Babs,' he soothed her. 'Come with us. We're just nipping out for a quick drink.'

Caspar was furious. Quick drink! Quick *fuck* had been the plan, and William knew it. Round to the Partridge, stroll across the lawn, behind the rooster hedge, and under the low brushing arms of the cypress. He almost went into spasm at the thought, but bloody Barbara was off on some new spasm of her own.

'*Where*? *Where* are you going for your drink? Tell me! *Tell* me!'

Startled, William dropped his sister's arm.

'Why? What's the matter?'

And Barbara stamped her foot. Caspar was fascinated. He'd never seen anyone, even a child, actually do it before. But Barbara lifted one of the great puffy columns under her skirt, and thumped it down on the floor tiles.

'Tell me *where*!'

'For God's sake, Barbara! Next door, of course.'

'No!'

William, who knew her better, got there first.

30

'Oh, I see! That's where he *is*, isn't it? Next door. You don't want us round there because that's where he works, your famous Miguel.'

'Miguel-*Angel*!'

'Miguel-Angel,' William conceded to keep the peace. Once again, he started patting his sister. 'Oh, come on, Barbara. Don't be so coy. Tell us about him. How long has he been there? What does he do? Is he a waiter, or a manager, or what?'

'Mostly he works in the garden,' said Barbara sullenly, after a pause.

Goodbye, sweet fuck, thought Caspar.

'Gardening? Or fetching drinks?'

'All right!' snapped Barbara. 'He's a *waiter*.' But, once it was out, she clearly felt better. In fact she smiled. 'Of course, he's not *really* a waiter. He's just brushing up the language, and getting a bit of experience. From what he says, I don't think he'll be a waiter very long.'

Snob, Caspar thought. Silly fat overblown snob. And then he realized that Barbara, to be fair, was at a disadvantage on this one. She didn't have Caspar's intimate (and plentiful) experience of waiters. And it was probably hard for her to keep Mrs Collett's almost inevitable reaction out of mind, and prevent it from colouring her assumptions about the judgement of others.

'But I *like* waiters,' teased William. 'I always have done.' Brazenly, he turned to Caspar. 'How about you?'

Whenever William grinned, Caspar was lost.

'Yes. I like waiters, too.'

William turned back to his sister.

'So that makes three of us.'

And suddenly, at last, Barbara calmed down. Her body

softened and her little moon face broke into her first real smile. Laying a plump paw on her brother's arm, she told him:

'You're not to go round there. Promise? Not till I've introduced you, anyway.'

'Why? Don't you trust this Miguel-Angel of yours?'

'Of course I trust him.'

'Is it us, then? Don't you trust us?'

'I don't have to trust you,' Barbara said with dignity. 'That's not an issue. And, if it were, I wouldn't want to get married.'

'Well, what is it? Why can't Caspar and I slip round to the Partridge for a little drink?'

'Because I don't want him to meet you there, that's why. Not while he's working. I want him to meet you *here*, and wearing his own clothes, not in some silly waiter's uniform with toggles and epaulettes. I want him to *meet* you, not serve you. Don't you see?'

'I see,' said Caspar, and this time he did.

7

Behind the Kaiser Wilhelm moustache

It didn't stop him wanting to go round there, though. In fact, it made things worse. Visions of toggles and epaulettes danced in his brain, making him dizzy with lust as he recalled the boy from – where was it, Prague? Budapest? – he'd managed to inveigle behind the goat pen after some circus show. 'Why goats?' he'd asked, more for something to say than from any real curiosity, and the boy had mimed drinking. Up until then, Caspar had never realized a group of travellers could be quite so cosily self-contained – something brought home to him again a few minutes later when his cooperative new friend made it quite clear he had to go: they would be missing him inside the caravan. But that was not before he'd let Caspar push off the worn green jacket with its glittering fringes, and free the billowing sleeves. It was like standing face to face with Robin Hood. And when Caspar slid his hands inside the tight trousers, he realized, with a charge that fixed the early coupling in his memory, that there was nothing there but cool hard bum. Not everyone had a mother, then. Not everyone's underwear was whipped away, and brought back a few days later, fresh-smelling and in neat piles. Some men could be unzipped and –

Defeated by yet another visceral surge of lust, Caspar tacked sideways out of Barbara's wake, abandoning the coffee cups he was carrying at the foot of some tall but ruthlessly pruned fern. Slipping up the back stairs, he made his way into William's old room through the unused second bathroom. Inside the trunk under the window he found the bag of ancient dressing-up clothes still stuffed on top of the old toys and jigsaws. Really, of course, he ought to have returned the sultan's costume they'd stolen last time so William could give him a cheap thrill. And the French beret. And that black cloak with sewn-on silver stars. The bag was looking altogether depleted, in fact. So who would even notice the further loss of one disintegrating false moustache? Picking the glitter from a pair of angel's wings off its frayed tufts, Caspar pressed the pitifully wilting thing to his upper lip. Promptly, it fell off. Holding it back in place with his free hand, he rooted through the clutter silting up the sides of the trunk and, sure enough, soon found the little tube. The glue in it had dried so hard he had to bite off the nozzle. Then, moving across to William's triptych of mirrors (and how, with three sisters, had he snaffled *that*?), Caspar twisted the ends back in some semblance of their original shape, and stuck the whole thing on his face.

'*Sehr gut,*' he told the stranger behind the Kaiser Wilhelm moustache. Then it was back down the stairs, out of the side door, and along the row of dustbins.

Over the wall.

8

'Fat chance!'

'Look!'

Tory stepped out of the larder. 'What?'

Gillyflower didn't turn from the window.

'Caspar, scrambling over the wall.'

'Really?' Tory moved back to the table. 'Off for a drink, I suppose.' Unfolding the bag, she spooned flour into the bowl. 'I still can't work out if he's a bad influence on Will, or if we ought to be grateful.'

'He must make tons of money,' Gilly said wistfully, thinking of Angus at Horridge's.

Tory's mouth tightened.

'I wouldn't want to go to someone like him.'

Gillyflower drew back her hand from the swirls of apple peel littering the table.

'What do you mean?'

'You know,' Tory said sternly.

'No, I don't. Go on. Tell me.'

Tory rested her floured hands on the edge of the pastry bowl. 'I mean I think there's something a bit sick about not liking women enough to want to go to bed with them, but having your fingers up them all day for a living.'

Gilly gave it a moment's thought.

'What about women gynaecologists? That's the same, surely?'

'It's not the same at all. What would be comparable would be if a lesbian chose to specialize in proctology.'

35

'I suppose you're right,' Gilly said, though Tory would have put money on her sister not knowing if proctology was penises or arseholes. All that ever mattered to Gilly was paddling away from argument as soon as possible. Indeed, she was already at it. 'What was that funny story Will kept telling us about the gynaecologist who –'

'*I* don't know.' The resurrection of old tales was tiresome enough, and Tory certainly wasn't going to be waylaid by one. She gave her sister a look. 'Isn't one bad joke a day enough for you?'

Gillyflower lowered her voice.

'Do you mean Barbara?'

Tory pounded her pastry.

'Of course I mean Barbara. For heaven's sake! What are we going to do?'

'Do?'

'Yes, *do*,' Tory mimicked. 'What are we going to do to stop daft old Barbara making an idiot of herself again, and getting her heart broken into the bargain?'

'You don't *know* that,' said Gillyflower. 'Her Miguel-Angel might be nice. They might get married and live happily ever after and have a dozen children trailing after them.'

'Barbara is nearly forty!'

'Well, one or two, then.'

'And pigs might fly. And George might win the pools. And Mother might move into one of those nice new bungalows at the end of Frosthole Close.'

'I suppose so,' said Gilly. But Tory could tell from the wistful tone of her voice that she was not disposed to give up Barbara's dream so easily. Victoria felt like kicking her. How could she even pretend to have forgotten that fiasco four years ago, with Andrew Taylor from the Esso garage? And Bernard, before that, when it looked as if Barbara was simply not prepared to accept the fact that even a forceful man can change his mind. In the end, everyone was forced to speak to her quite sharply. You couldn't *drag* a partner to the altar, after all. And there was no point in waylaying them accidentally on purpose on practically every street corner. It wasn't as if people didn't notice.

'Third time lucky, perhaps,' Gillyflower said hopefully.

'Fat chance!' scoffed Tory, echoing the twins' parrotings from some American television show. Then, realizing what she'd said, she blushed, and quickly got on with her pastry.

9

Was there ever a time . . .?

'Come with me for a minute, would you, dear?'

'I was just −'

'It won't take long.'

William was even keener than usual not to go down the garden with his mother. For one thing, Caspar had disappeared. Had he slid off next door? For another, his mother was bound to start ripping up clumps of flowerbeds, and William couldn't stand watching it. And, for a third, he knew she wanted to have a chat about Barbara.

Sure enough:

'I'm so worried about your sister.'

William still prided himself on never going down without a fight.

'Who, Tory? Or do you mean Gillyflower?'

The first handful of campanula came out so fast, a spray of soil hit him in the face.

'Don't be silly. I'm talking about Barbara.'

'Oh, yes,' said William. 'Barbara. Splendid news. I'm sure he'll be nice, and I hope they'll be wonderfully happy.'

Was it from spite she chose the most attractive knot of flowers to rip out of the earth next? To save the garden, William settled down.

'So what's the problem?'

'Oh, Will!' Mrs Collett put her hand in the small of her back, and made a show of straightening. 'I don't know what's for the best. I'd love to put on a bit of a splash for poor Barbara. But think how dreadful it would be if anything went wrong this time.'

'This time?'

She made an effort not to snap at him. But typical of William, of course, to have forgotten that business with Mr Taylor from the filling station. Not to mention the other time, with that awful, bossy Bernard.

'This isn't your sister's first engagement, you know.'

'I don't think she is actually engaged. I think she's just planning on getting hitched.'

Was there ever a time, thought Mrs Collett, reaching down for more campanula, when her offspring didn't get on her nerves? Stolid, grinding, moralistic Victoria. Always there. Always right. In twenty years there hadn't been a war or an election without Tory sanctimoniously and successfully predicting the outcome, a household substance about which she wasn't fully apprised of the dangers, or any way of spending money or time of which she didn't somehow disapprove. 'What's in this lavatory cleaner? Is it *lye*?' 'You shouldn't buy the children tickets for that circus, Mother. Not while they still force animals to perform.' She stumped round the house on her ghastly once-a-month visits, pointing out patches of damp and sagging guttering exactly the same way she used to march round as a child, mercilessly dragging Lilith's attention back to her job as a mother. 'Will won't do his homework properly.' 'I think Gilly's crying.' 'Is supper going to be late?'

In comparison you couldn't complain about Gilly. But, try as she might, Mrs Collett couldn't help finding her youngest daughter's blend of sheer anxiousness to please and lack of spunk annoyed her even more. That Gillyflower was the nicest of her children, everyone was agreed. She meant well. She made a point of thinking the best of everyone, and never was first to prick a bubble by pointing out what might go wrong. People like Gilly were supposed to be pleasant company. But in Mrs Collett's experience, nice people were just *weak*. Morally bereft. They sailed through life, not bothering to make the efforts other people make to work out what is right and what is wrong, and go along with that. They simply did whatever caused the least trouble. Their only maxim seemed to be: avoid making waves. And so, of course, you couldn't depend on them for a moment. Not for anything. The line they took was so entirely consequential on who was beside them at the time, and in what mood, that they were wholly unpredictable. Each time Mrs Collett heard Gillyflower saying to someone, 'I suppose you're right,' she itched to slap her face. The hospital wards of Great Britain were probably filled to bursting because nice people like Gilly were more concerned with avoiding unpleasantness than with taking a firm stand about things like drunken guests not driving home, or children walking as far as the traffic lights to cross the road at a safe place. And why should the rest of us have to struggle through life trying to work out what's best and who's right, when people like Gillyflower could sail through without any of the nuisance of moral backbone, and even find themselves admired for it? 'But she's so easy-going!' 'She's so *nice*!'

The next clump that came out was practically the size of Mrs Collett's head.

'Steady on,' William warned, 'or you'll have the whole lot up.'

What business was it of his? He was hardly well known for his offers of help in the garden. What gave him the right to criticize? It was astonishing, thought Mrs Collett, just how much horticultural advice was offered by people with soft hands. They clearly had absolutely no idea what sort of effort it took to keep a garden as large as this one in control. Just as the childless, of course, never had any idea how much work went into raising a family. One hurdle after another. One grim, continual grind that started one day almost as if by accident, and went on thirty years. What did people without children know about going months and months unable to sit and enjoy a meal for having to think forward to the next one? Of not having the option, even for a single day, of ignoring the shopping, or cooking, or washing, or cleaning? Just having to keep at it. And not even being able to listen to the radio as you drudged, what with doorbells and telephones forever interrupting, and things needing carrying from one end of the house to the other. Why, even if you settled to something in one room, like mending or getting the supper, some child would be bound to appear within seconds, wanting to chat, or asking for help with their homework. Practically as far back as she could remember, Lilith had hated every minute of mothering. And like some dreadful form of allergy, it had got worse and worse, until she could hardly do anything, anything at all, without resenting how much being the linchpin of a family ruined it. Everything was spoiled, somehow. She didn't know how other women managed to stay sane, let alone pleasant, when they couldn't even unwrap their own Christmas gifts without secretly calculating if a judicious bit of tactful recycling now might claw back a few precious moments eleven months in the future – save them from one more trip down the bloody shops. Oh, fine for William to stand there looking so pained at the way she was gardening. When had he ever had to rush through one task in order to get on with the next, and the next, and the mountain of tasks after that? Why, by the time she was his age she had a house, a husband, and four children. What did William have? Nothing. Not a single responsibility. And he even had someone to look after him! Her children certainly knew how to fall on their feet . . .

'Mother! There'll be none left at this rate!'

What on earth was he on about? Oh, the wretched campanula. As if it mattered.

'It's your sister you should be worrying about. Not the flowerbeds.'

'But *why*?'

He didn't expect an answer, and none came. After a moment, tipping back his head, he let the sunlight that speckled through the branches fill his eyes till they watered, then squeezed them, to make rainbows. It was a childish thing to do, but this whole performance reminded him of grisly childhood – her bent over, stabbing furiously with a trowel, him standing around, forever trying to think of answers to her mad questions: 'Why do you *think* I'm cross?' 'What do you *think* you've done to upset me?' Once, flicking through channels on the television, he'd come across a brash American mother with her hands on her pink-trousered hips, telling a child, 'I'm mad as hell because you broke that bottle. You can just pay for the next one out of your allowance, and go and fetch it now.' The sheer simplicity of the announcement had struck him so forcibly he'd had to switch off and sit for a few moments, thinking. Was there ever a time he hadn't been expected to work out for himself, through hours of icy, punishing silence, just what his crime had been, and how he was expected to make reparation? And now, to realize that this particular way of bringing young sinners to book was optional! How did Tory bring up her children? How would Gillyflower? To think that discipline, like education or diet, was simply a matter of someone's decision, a choice between alternate ways. Why, all over the world, parents were probably leaning over the cradle, thinking about the difference between what they'd received and what they wanted to pass on, and whispering to their first-born, 'One thing I promise you I'll never, ever do is −'

Red alert! No doubt exasperated by his faraway expression, she'd turned her back on him. What was she pulling out now? He couldn't see unless he moved round beside her, and he couldn't do that unless he thought of something to say. Otherwise it would look as if he were spying on her weeding. Except, of course, that it was never just weeds she was after. It was the body of the garden: its rich ground cover and its trailing growths, its heavy burgeoning knots of green, studded with bright red −

'Mother! Not the aubrietia!'

She turned on him in a fury.

'Mind your own business, William!'

But it *was*. It *was* his business. He'd lived in this garden. He'd grown up in it. He felt at bay, watching her uproot and prune, thin out and pare. Why couldn't she leave the place to grow and thrive and spread and swarm till − till *what*? Oh, face it. Caspar said it often enough, and he was probably right. Till it wasn't her garden any longer, but *his* again, as it had been all through childhood, when she, too busy even to lift her myriad tools of destruction, had left it to turn to its own purposes. Till it ran riot, and,

43

floored with tangled greenery, raftered with creepers and dense with foliage, was once more impregnable and perfect, with brambles smothering all the ghastly past, and briars strangling memory.

He let the sunlight flood his eyes till they spilled over. Oh, dream on, William. That'll be the day.

10

Under these very bushes . . .

'Mind your own business, William!'

Caspar, leaning against the other side of the wall, heard the sharp reprimand and smiled. Mistake. The false moustache gave up its already enfeebled grip on his upper lip, and fell off in his lap. Caspar rolled it in a ball, and shoved it away in his pocket. It had already served its purpose, anyway. He'd seen Miguel-Angel de Whatsit. He'd bought a cocktail (and a couple of spares). The wall felt warm against his back, the sun shone, and, as he idly stirred the crushed ice in his drink with the tiny paper umbrella, Caspar was perfectly happy. Miguel-Angel was, contrary to expectation, a real treat. Crush-bummed and lithe as any glittering matador . . . And obviously straight. But never mind. Barbara deserved good fortune. His feelings warmed to expansiveness by brief escape, his second cocktail and a cloudless sky, Caspar wished everyone good fortune. Here was the place for it, after all. It was under these very bushes that he'd met William – well, not *met* him, exactly. They'd met in the bar, of course. Lost between Fellaham and the motorway after an unsuccessful attempt to shave a few miles off the drive back to London, Caspar had called in at the Partridge for a quick half, and directions. William, togged up in his waiter's finery, was trolling up and down behind the bar – flashing smiles, dropping coins, 'Will there be anything else, sir?' His shift hadn't finished till three, and by then Caspar (more sobered than William by their near discovery in the handicapped lavatory) had still been far too drunk to drive. So they'd spent the rest of the afternoon under these very rhododendrons. The purpley-blue one, recalled Caspar, writhing through one of the frequent visceral seizures with which the sexual geography of his relationship with William seemed to have littered his life. (He could barely drive down Longley Street now without crashing.) William would do — had done — anything. Caspar was almost shocked, certainly bruised, and, in one or two places, fairly badly skinned. He'd driven back the following evening for more. And the next. And the next. As soon as he found out that his beautiful boy tramp simply went home from work by scrambling over the wall, he'd begged to shift the venue of their couplings. 'It would be safer, surely. Your mother can't garden all *night*.'

But William was adamant. So they'd stuck to doing it among the rhododendrons of the Partridge. Not once in all those first few glorious days — or since — had they done it over the wall, on hallowed ground. In the house, yes. Over the last five years, Caspar had pulled William between sheets and into wardrobes. He'd pushed him against walls, over sofa backs, and on to his knees behind conservatory doors. The very words 'Where's Mother?' now worked like a charm to give Caspar instant erection. But maybe because she was so often down the garden, they'd never done it there.

'Today's the day,' Caspar muttered firmly. Tipping his head back, he poured the last of Cocktail No. 2 down his throat. Lovely. Yum, yum. William was mad about Moosewood Tailwaggers. And after being snarled at, he'd need a drink. Their first fling in the garden coming up, then. Virgin turf. With Cocktail No. 3 held out before him as a bribe, William would surely not resist.

11

A perfect stranger

William resisted.

He told Caspar clearly enough, while Mrs Collett was in the potting shed, finding a sharper trowel.

'No,' he said. 'Maybe back in the house, later. But not here. Not now.'

Caspar leaned dangerously far over the wall, waving Cocktail No. 3 from side to side like an oddly shaped censer.

'No,' William hissed. (Mrs Collett was on her way back now, delaying only long enough to rip out a couple of impertinent fritillaries.)

'We could go round behind the greenhouse . . .'

William didn't bother to respond.

'Down in the shrubbery? Behind the sycamore? Under that big bush next to the tennis court?'

'Flowering currant,' William said automatically, but he showed no signs of cracking.

'At the bottom of the scullery steps? Up by the end wall?'

'No!'

'On top of the compost heap? In the lily pond? Down the well?'

(Caspar was getting silly now.)

'Go away,' William told him. 'I'm having a private conversation with my mother.'

'No, you're not.'

'Yes, I am.'

And suddenly, once again, he was. Mrs Collett materialized between the azaleas and, just as if she hadn't been away, took up the business of Barbara and the wedding.

'Your sister sails in, without a single word of warning, and kindly informs us she plans to get married to a perfect stranger . . .'

Caspar sank out of sight behind the wall, clutching the unfinished cocktail. A perfect stranger. Yes. Exactly so. That was about what he was. Caspar had sidled through the hotel's ever-open front door, affecting to stroke the moustache in whose adhesive powers he had so little faith. Almost at once, a busy little man had swept across the hall, saying to Caspar as he ushered him towards another doorway, 'Mr Hamill from the council?' Caspar's attempt to disassociate himself from this suggestion turned, with a bit of help from the recalcitrant moustache, into what could as easily have been an embarrassed nod, and before he could put things straight, the busy little man was already on his way out. 'I'll fetch the rest of the papers. Just a tick.'

Caspar gambled on the tick concerned giving him enough time to stick the moustache on straight again before slipping out across the hallway and into the darkest recess of the bar. But he was out of luck. A tap on the door was followed almost instantly by its opening.

'Drink, sir?'

The accent was Spanish, but Caspar didn't dare look up. By now, the moustache had parted company from his upper lip, and was nestling comfortably on his fingers. Caspar bent over the table, pretending he was absorbed in the paperwork spread before him.

'Could you do me a Moosewood Tailwagger?' he asked hopefully.

In the stricken silence that followed, Caspar's eyes focused. '*Application for planning permission to build seven chalet-style hotel accommodation units*,' he read. And, two lines further down, '*Name and address of landowner: Mrs Moira Lilith Collett, Cold Domain, Little Furley, near Fellaham.*'

'Moose –? Moose –?'

Miguel-Angel was clearly seriously at sea.

Suddenly, the moustache stuck firmly to Caspar's fingers. Thank God! At last, by accident, he'd found a seam of fairly active glue. Ruthlessly twisting the moustache to take advantage of this face-saver, Caspar pushed it on again. This time it stayed in place. Quickly he turned to face his interlocutor, not reckoning to find himself instantly thrown again by stunning good looks. Before him Miguel-Angel stood – tall and dark-eyed, with just that look of brooding fierceness Caspar associated with weakening pleasures.

'Oh, blimey!' breathed Caspar, just the way, forty years earlier, he'd let out the same soft exclamation on opening *Great Renaissance Paintings*. 'Oh, blimey!'

'Moose –?'

The glorious Spaniard was still struggling.

Caspar got a grip.

'A Moosewood Tailwagger,' he said again. 'We'll need some lime, but basically it's two parts gin and one part . . .'

Striding across (almost the military man with his moustache), he ushered Miguel-Angel out of the room just as he himself had been so opportunely ushered in.

'Come on,' he said. 'Back to the bar. I'll show you.'

I 2

A perfect Gillyflower . . . a real shit

Over lunch, Barbara was put through the third degree.

'And shall you have a list, dear?'

'A list?'

'For gifts.'

'Oh. Yes. I suppose so. I don't know.'

'And will his parents come?'

'I should think so.'

'All the way from Spain?'

Caspar could almost hear the light 'Fancy!' at the end. So this was how Mrs Collett reeled her children back after a flurry of unpleasantness: by presenting them with a series of mild little questions to which it would seem childish, even churlish, not to reply.

'You haven't met his parents yet, then?'

'No, not yet.'

'They haven't managed to come over and visit him?'

'He's only been here three months.'

Oh, Barbara! Caspar could see it on every face round the table. Oh, Barbara! Oh, Barbara! Oh, Barbara!

'It isn't very long, dear . . .'

'It's long enough.'

'I expect you know best.'

This last was said with such a transparent lack of conviction that even stern Tory felt sorry enough for her sister to cause a diversion.

'You haven't any wine, Babs!'

William compounded the sympathy by pushing across the table the bottle of fizzy water Barbara had sent him to the shop to buy.

'I haven't really stopped drinking,' Barbara told everyone. 'It's only the calories. I have to get into a wedding dress, don't forget. I'd just like to look more like a tent than a big top.'

But no one, not even soppy Gillyflower, would let her talk about her wedding finery. Resolutely, the conversation was steered away, first to mineral waters, then, by way of the iniquities of water companies, to the parlous state of many of Britain's beaches. Someone as fat as Barbara, Caspar thought, came up against exactly the same brick walls that he and William faced, where discussions were sidetracked, interesting discussions were sent up blind alleys, and every effort was made to paddle clear of things that others didn't want to think about: a great roly-poly woman stepping out of virginal white, and going at it; men loving other men. Quick! Turn the table talk to the high price of mineral water and all the problems of its home delivery. Talk about turds floating up on to beaches. Anything, no matter how boring or disgusting, rather than the mysteries of fat flesh or queer flesh. But everyone's sex life was a mystery – as much to the person concerned as to any outsider. Caspar could still not explain how one unsatisfactory quarter of an hour with that unwashed youth from Weston-Super-Mare could have come to haunt so many daydreams and be the prop of so much fantasy. What were a few yards of slimy seaweed, after all, that they could –

'Caspar?'

He dragged his attention back. What had they moved

on to now? Nitrates in the water table? European Economic Community Directives?

'Caspar, you've been married. During the ceremony, whose job is it to –'

Bitch! Queen Bitch Victoria! Through visit after visit she'd stolidly buttressed her mother's quite impenetrable social stockade against all mention of his personal life, rendering him practically *mute*. Then, as soon as it suited her, she broke her own bloody rule! Well, freeze her out, for starters.

'Not sure I can remember, Tory. So long ago . . .'

But Mrs Collett was on it in a flash. It was, after all, grist to her theme that getting married could turn out to be a terrible mistake.

'I didn't know you had a wife, Caspar.'

'I don't. However, Victoria is correct. I was once married.'

Though how she knew was beyond him. Unless . . .

Yes. William was looking reproachfully at Barbara. And Barbara, rumbled in indiscretion, was biting her lip in guilt. But never mind that now. Time enough to take that up with the two of them later. Now it was time to see off the enemy.

'And I have a son,' he announced, putting as much pride as he could muster into the mention of that sullen, intermittently grasping oaf who gave 'learning to coppice' as the pretext for sharing a caravan in Northumberland with two long-legged West Indian beauties. 'His name is Joshua.'

'How old is he?' Tory asked instantly.

A bloody sight too close to William's age for Caspar not to lie. And, as the world and his wife know, once you start lying it is hard to stop.

'He works for a very fine computer software company on the south coast. Currently, he's in the divisional management development section, but in the longer term –'

All through the fruit salad and the cheese, he bored them back, taking revenge for Tory's spite (and all that tiresome drivel about mineral waters and dirty beaches) by telling them at interminable length, and in tones of paralysing tedium, about some other quite invented son, his boring job, his utterly common or garden flat, his unremarkable car. Each time he noticed anyone's attention flagging, he promptly reeled them back in. 'That's the interesting thing about computers, Gillyflower . . .' 'I expect you know that part of the country, Mrs Collett. Well, if you drive east a little way . . .' 'As you may have read in the papers, Victoria, the sheer acceleration capacity of that range of hatchback . . .' William just stared in mesmerized horror. But Barbara, soft soul that she was, appeared to be truly riveted. On the only occasion on which he fell momentarily silent, startling himself half to death by reaching in his pocket for his handkerchief and closing his fingers instead round the furry ends of the forgotten moustache, she burst in, scarcely able to contain herself.

'And did Joshua choose all those mushroom carpets and beige walls himself? Or did he have someone to advise him?'

'Sorry?'

Caspar was faltering suddenly. He'd made the mistake of glancing towards Mrs Collett, and this time the animosity in her eyes was unmistakable. Had he pushed his luck too far? Did she suspect, if only from the look on William's face, that he was making the whole boiling up, playing games with them at their own table? Not that she'd ever trusted him. Right from the start she'd made it plain that it was Caspar whom she held to blame for William's fall from grace. Oh, it must have been obvious, even to someone as cocooned in self-absorption as Mrs Collett, that her son was no innocent. He had dabbled before. But in leaving home to set up with another man, he'd taken degradation one step further. He'd made his depravity (and her failure) public. And Caspar was the villain. He was quite obviously, after all, the more powerful of the two. He had better suits, more money, a luxurious car – and he was twenty years older. A woman of her sort would be bound to think that it was Caspar who made all the moves, called all the shots. From there it would be the smallest of leaps to conclude that, without this sexual Svengali at his side, her William might by now have grown out of the least understandable, the most repellent, of all his unfortunate phases. Might have grown up and married. Properly.

No wonder she didn't like him. And Caspar suddenly realized how very much he didn't like her back. There she sat, her lips pinched with disapproval, her fingers picking at imaginary threads. What right had she to look at him that way? She'd let him in on sufferance. Allowed him, so long as he behaved himself, to sit at the fringes of her family. He had been graciously permitted to take time he could ill afford away from his clinical responsibilities several times a year in order to chauffeur her ungrateful son down to this godforsaken backwater, to visit her. But only on her terms. No mention of their true relationship. No reference to their London life. Even Caspar's prestigious field of work was, here, forbidden ground in case conversation stemming from the subject should lead, as well it might, on to the perilous topic of natural human behaviour. No, Caspar was supposed to sit quietly and unassumingly in his chair, look pleasant, and agree with everyone. And pass the sugar when they asked him.

Well, bugger her. In fact, bugger the whole bloody family. Look at them, fawning round, being careful, guarding their tongues, forever on watch for her next mood as though they were helpless little children in thrall to some wicked stepmother for the roof over their heads and their next crust. He'd show the whole pack of them. Oh, yes, he would! How many times had he driven William down to this ghastly House of Hell? Well over a dozen, surely. And every time he'd been as good as gold. Sat tight, and obeyed the rules, just like the rest of them. A perfect Gillyflower! Well, not today. Not with three of Miguel-Angel's Moosewood Tailwaggers and half a bottle of her cheap Chardonnay swilling around inside him. He'd had enough. If she and that pickle-up-the-arse daughter of hers suddenly felt free to open the Pandora's box of his past life and family, then he could bloody well open theirs. And what was in it? Well, apparently an application for planning permission for seven chalet-style hotel units in the garden, for starters. Watch your back, Mrs Collett. You're in trouble now.

Pushing his chair back, Caspar turned to Barbara.

'I'll carry those for you.'

'I'm fine, really.'

'No, please. Let me.'

He prised the pile of dishes from her hands, and followed her out of the room. While Barbara was struggling with the antiquated coffee machine that Mrs Collett made a point of preferring to any of the new ones her daughters had bought her, Caspar laid a hand on her shoulder.

'Barbara.'

She swung round, startled by his touch.

'Barbara, I have to ask you a favour.'

'Oh, Caspar!' There was relief on her face. (What on earth had she expected?) 'Anything, Caspar. You know that.'

'Anything?'

She spread her hands.

'If I can.'

'Then promise me you'll let me book you a wedding bash at the Partridge.'

'Next door?'

She was confused.

'Yes.' Caspar took both her hands in his. 'Listen, Barbara. You wanted your wedding party in the garden here. Well, think. Half the lawn's overshadowed by that great sycamore. And so is half next door. So let's just shift the festivities to the other side. You'll be under the very same tree. Each time you look up, it will almost be the same.'

Her look of hope was almost pitiful.

'Under the same tree . . .'

'Exactly so.'

She suddenly looked anxious.

'But, Caspar! What about Miguel-Angel?'

'I'm sure he'd be pleased,' Caspar said firmly. 'In fact, there's something rather nice about celebrating at his place of work. He'll have a few more supporters.'

'I suppose he would.'

She was halfway to daydreaming already, Caspar could tell.

'But the expense!'

He squeezed her hands warmly before letting them go.

'My pleasure,' he told her, truthfully.

'Do you really mean that?'

Caspar smiled.

'Come on, Barbara,' he jollied her. 'Look at me. Do I look as if a *wedding* could put me in Queer Street?'

She burst out laughing. He had won his case.

'I'm delighted,' he told her. 'And William will be thrilled. Absolutely thrilled.'

Again, she looked anxious.

'What about Mother, though?'

Caspar feigned innocence.

'Your mother? Surely she'll be delighted too. She won't have any of the worry or the stress, but she'll have the pleasure of knowing how happy it makes you and Miguel-Angel.'

'Oh, Caspar! You must meet him!'

'Yes, I must.'

All through the loading of the coffee tray, she chattered on. Guests. Seating arrangements. Awnings. Canapés. Caspar didn't bother to listen. Carrying the sugar bowl and the jug of milk she handed him, he followed her back to the table, the perfect innocent, and took his seat to watch the fireworks.

'Mother –'

'Nothing in mine, dear, except the tiniest splash of milk.'

Barbara passed the coffee, exactly as ordered, up the table. And then she tried again.

'Mother, I think Caspar's solved our little problem for us.'

'Problem?'

Mrs Collett's expression gave the world to understand she was not aware of having any problem.

'About where we have my wedding.'

'Ah, yes.'

The distaste was plain.

'We're having it next door.'

'Next door?'

Clearly, the significance of this did not sink in at once. Mrs Collett looked mystified.

'You don't mean at the *Partridge*?' Tory said, disbelieving. 'A glass of *water* at the Partridge costs the earth. You couldn't possibly afford to have a reception there.'

Barbara turned to Caspar, her face aglow with fondness and gratitude.

'Caspar has kindly offered –'

'Oh, really!'

Mrs Collett gripped the tablecloth. The nearest coffee cups jerked closer, slopping their murky contents overboard on to her perfect linen. She didn't even notice. The sheer physical effort of trying to suppress the depth of the irritation she felt drained the blood from her face.

'Caspar, don't you think this is really a *private* matter? Something best discussed amongst those it concerns?'

Caspar shrugged, and said amicably, 'I like to think of myself as family.' He patted Gillyflower's hand. 'You think of me as family, don't you, Gillyflower?'

Gillyflower blushed, but, watching her mother's face, she didn't dare answer. William suppressed a snigger born more of nerves than amusement. And Tory, as usual, chose to round sharply on her sister.

'Barbara, you shouldn't even have let Caspar offer. It's ridiculous. For one thing, it would cost a fortune –'

'I don't mind,' Caspar interrupted. 'And if I don't mind, surely nobody else should.'

He said this staring at Mrs Collett with open curiosity. Did she suspect that he had somehow found out about her plans for the garden? Unlikely. If she thought that, she would be angrier. She would be off the wall. She must still be assuming that this was a snippet of bad luck, a mere bedevilling coincidence that could be seen off promptly and easily with just a few words to her busy little co-conspirator over the wall. 'And it would make things so much easier if I don't have my family breathing down my neck through all this business. Naturally, they're senti-mental about the garden. After all, they grew up here, and seeing such a chunk of it going to make your lovely new chalets will be like watching their happy, happy childhood being uprooted. I honestly believe the less time they have to brood, the better. So if, by chance . . .' And Barbara's booking would be inexorably refused: '. . . regret to inform you . . . not a single free date . . .'

Yes. Here it came.

'You mustn't build up your hopes, dear. Everyone says they're very busy indeed at the Partridge. I've heard of one or two couples already who have been disappointed.'

'Really?' said Gillyflower, curious. 'Who's getting mar-ried round here?'

'I don't think you know them, dear.'

'I might,' said William. 'I met a lot of people when I was working there. What are they called?'

She didn't answer. Indeed, it looked to Caspar as if she was suddenly at a loss for any further invention. She looked more rattled and distressed than he had ever seen her. He was astonished. He hadn't thought he'd done much more than make a small move in the family game of chess. After all, he told himself, if she'd the nerve to crown her

usual horticultural gouge and shred with this extraordinary *tour de force* – the total razing of her offspring's
childhood Arcadia – then surely she had the bottle to tell
them. If it weren't for the fact that he'd have to come
clean about the false moustache and meeting Miguel-
Angel, he'd do it for her. Imagine their reaction!

And suddenly, belatedly, Caspar imagined it. Tory, of
course, would go berserk on ecological grounds alone.
He'd heard her views on thoroughly unsuitable modern
developments plonked, willy-nilly, in the middle of old
villages. Not that she had a high opinion of the Partridge
anyway. She was forever griping on about things Caspar
never even noticed, like car doors slamming late at night,
and cocktail umbrellas stuck for a joke in the front hedge.
Barbara would throw one of her giant wobblies. She'd
burst into disgusting tears, and no doubt start going on
about the dozens of small, furry, once-beloved things she
seemed to have buried all over the garden. Caspar had
taken a turn around it with her once, and every few
moments, so it seemed, she'd interrupted herself, (more
rarely, him) to intone reverently: 'That's Monty's grave,'
or, 'Tweety's buried under that magnolia.' After a while,
he'd had the sense that anywhere he put his feet, he might
hear the crunch of breastbone or the squelch of rotted fur.

But William! William's response didn't bear thinking
about. If William had one overriding gift, it was for
unflagging hysteria. He'd make a tremendous and immediate scene – well, fair enough. But even after he'd stormed
from the house and locked himself in the Rover, he'd keep
it up. The whole journey back to London. The whole
night. And then for days, weeks – as long as the chalet-
building business took. It might be *months*. And even

afterwards. Caspar knew William, and he knew his hates. He'd seen a couple of them already firsthand, but never anything that mattered. Nothing like this. This would be terrible. It would be unimaginably grim. A period of quite intolerable misery. There'd be no other topic of conversation. None. Caspar's exhausted responses would be suspiciously sifted, deemed inadequate, and all the anger banked up against Mrs Collett and her plans would crash down on Caspar time and time again.

And Caspar couldn't stand it. He knew his limitations, and it would be the end of him and William. The final showdown would no doubt turn out to be something quite trivial, about which William could condemn him afterwards to their few mutual friends: Caspar's refusal to fund some further, futile trawl of legal advice, or his unwillingness to waste yet another whole day helping William chase it. But it would be a showdown none the less. William would start to pack his huge green holdall, as he had done a score of times before. But this time Caspar wouldn't be at his side, hauling the clothes out of the zippered compartments as fast as William could hurl them in. Caspar could see it coming. This time he'd sit back on the bed, and watch in real relief as, after weeks of seething argument and tears and sleepless nights, William went off for good.

Is that what he wanted? To have the steady tenor of his days disrupted utterly over a garden, the mere mention of which already infuriated him almost beyond endurance? Wasn't it enough that so many of his precious nights had been disturbed by William's never-ending dreams about the place? What was he thinking about, helping to precipitate a volcanic eruption that would rain misery on all their days, simply to spite this hunted, nonplussed woman desperately plucking at the chicken skin around her neck?

Caspar looked round the table. Barbara, still rapt with happiness, was patting the mound of flesh between her ribcage and the table top, and joking about how little time she had to get rid of it. William was cheerfully teasing her with some unlikely scenario in which she'd half faded away, and Gilly was giggling at the faces her sister was making, sipping coffee without milk or sugar. Even Tory, now she had temporarily ceded the responsibility of disapproval to her mother, had lost her usual look of stone.

And sobered, sobered utterly, Caspar sat and considered. Like Mrs Collett, he had reached a watershed. Like her, he faced on one side instant, outright pandemonium. And, on the other, the slim outside chance of just a few more weeks of peace, crowned by a brilliantly engineered *fait accompli* whereby these overgrown babes would, at last, get a boot out of the clinging greenery of their childhood wonderland, into the real world.

And, feeling a shit, a real shit, Caspar chose.

II

I

The years between them . . .

Restless, unable to sleep, Caspar reached down into the little pot kept ready by the bed. Rolling William away from him, on to his stomach, he gently slid his finger down between William's buttocks, then up again. Instantly William woke, and pushed the hand away, not to reject him but to switch their roles. Caspar submitted with pleasure and relief. One of the nicest things about William was that, boyish as he was, he still as often as not preferred to take the upper hand (if you could call it that). William said nothing, and he took his time. And though, afterwards, Caspar experimentally squeezed his shoulder once or twice, wondering if he wanted to talk, it was not until they were sitting opposite one another over breakfast the next morning that the subject of Thursday's communication from the Partridge finally came up between them.

'So,' William said, studying the monstrous quotation for the twentieth time. 'Not just a wedding in the family. A bankruptcy, too.'

'Looks like it.'

William began shunting spoons and marmalade jars and salt and pepper pots round in frenetic little circles.

'What I can't understand is why you had to offer to pay for it. And at the Partridge! You must have gone temporarily *unhinged*.'

Rather than have to put William straight about the

tell-tale papers he'd seen lying on the table, Caspar let this pass, only answering vaguely:

'Somebody had to be nice to Barbara.'

'But *you*!' William was shunting things round so fast now that there was bound to be an accident any moment. Caspar just hoped it wouldn't be the pepper pot, which was a rather poorly baked clay thing in the shape of a penis that Joshua had made, presumably as some sort of fond and knowing joke, after the separation. Caspar put out a hand to lift the memento of a younger, kinder son safely out of the spinning circle.

'Why not me?'

'Come off it,' William said sharply. 'Why should you bother about Barbara?' He narrowed his eyes at Caspar. 'I reckon if you hadn't sloped round there and spotted Miguel-Angel –'

'And drunk three of his Moosewood Tailwaggers,' Caspar reminded him.

William snorted. The marmalade came closer than ever to colliding with the salt, and Caspar reached out to remove it.

'Why shouldn't I do something for Barbara?' he asked. 'I'm fond of her.' And when William's only response was another contemptuous snort, Caspar couldn't help adding defensively, '*You're* fond of her.'

'I've reasons to be fond of her,' William said stonily. 'She's my sister. And she's been good to me. While all the rest of them were secretly wishing I'd disappear in a puff of smoke, and cringing with embarrassment whenever they had to introduce me to their friends, and making excuses to leave their precious little children at home, safe out of Uncle William's way, she always came up trumps.'

Caspar laid his own hand on one of the two still frenziedly pushing breakfast goodies round and round the table. He'd played straight so far into his own life (fooling himself for long enough, before taking even more care to fool others) that it always came as a shock to be reminded that the bitterest experiences for any younger lover were far more likely to stem from the occasions on which they'd disclosed the nature of their passions than the times when they'd had to conceal them. And so the world would, very likely, end up divided into those who took the news well, and those who didn't. Caspar himself could not forget how reasonable and brave Clara had been. Of course, over their twelve years together she'd had enough clues; and there had even been a couple of carefully glossed-over rows when he'd been caught, as she so hurtfully put it, 'slobbering over other men' before he had finally declared himself, and she'd walked out, taking Joshua with her. But it was somehow still a comfort to Caspar to know that, though he could not wipe out his own guilt and self-disgust at the stupidity that led him to deny his own feelings for so long, thereby derailing three lives, Clara herself hardly blamed him. 'Don't feel so bad. It probably would have happened anyway. Everyone gets divorced.'

'She was a real *brick*.'

Caspar broke his reverie to realize, with relief, that this apparent echo of his own thoughts was simply William pressing on with his own tale. 'Barbara was *brilliant*, right from the start. It was she who told Dad a few simple facts of life it turned out he didn't even *know*, and sent Gilly off to drag Mother back from wherever she'd rushed off down the garden, and told Tory to get on with stuffing the turkey —'

'You never told them all on Christmas Day!' (Truly, this coming-out stuff was a perfect curse. Suddenly Caspar felt a little better about leaving things till some dismal, dripping Sunday afternoon shortly after his fortieth birthday.)

Now William was glowering.

'What's wrong with that?'

'Nothing.' Hastily Caspar rose from the table and tipped his plate and knife into the sink. The years between them might have been a lifetime. Caspar could not regret passing as 'normal' in his daily life. It was the best way to protect his privacy, and Caspar was solitary and unforthcoming by nature. As young as six or seven, he knew which were his secrets, and how best to keep them. Once, as he sat beside his mother at the kitchen table, some man whose name and face he'd since forgotten entirely had pushed his chair back hard across the floor. 'Better get back,' he'd said regretfully. 'My fellow will be wondering where I am.' It was, for Caspar, an electric moment, though even now he'd no idea at all exactly what the visitor that morning was saying. Perhaps he'd just had a plumber waiting on the doorstep, or a tennis partner getting impatient as the minutes passed. It was, thought Caspar, typical of his young self that, though the words 'my fellow', spoken by a man, preoccupied him for weeks, he'd never asked his mother to explain. Not then or since. But, there again, he'd never discussed a single aspect of his way of life with any member of his family. And that had not been hard. Looking back, Caspar saw nothing but a chain of institutions, deaf and blind, all dedicated to not noticing that he was different in any way. Parents afraid to see, schools to admit, and colleagues to discuss. Everyone colluded to encourage his duplicity, and, as a result, it had taken Caspar years to put the pitiful and embarrassing fragments of his experience together, and face the real picture. It hadn't helped, of course, that women naturally gave their hearts to quiet men in white coats. To his dismay, he had repeatedly inspired affection in women who, unasked and unabashed, promptly laid claim to love. Part of the problem had always been Caspar's capacity for silence. The women round rushed in to fill the gaps with their self-binding confidences; then, to his horror, with their declarations; and, on the worst occasions, with demands. Each time he asked himself, 'What have I done?' And every time the answer was the same. His sheer lack of response had somehow, it seems, inspired his new acquaintance with even more confidence, rather than given her pause to think again. Each time it happened, Caspar was aghast to find that merely by being in this particular hospital, or on that committee, he had again stirred up in some poor woman feelings he couldn't return, desires he could never gratify. In this respect, his former marriage hung about him like a curse. He almost heard the whispered catechisms in the corridors as he walked by. 'Is he . . . you know?' 'No, I don't think so. He was married for years.' A single word in any place he'd been could have dispelled misunderstanding, saved Caspar awkwardness and others pain. But Caspar was incapable of saying it. How could a man his age, trained in the old world, step into the new? William could call him bourgeois and conformist, and hector him till hell froze about his responsibilities to a wider community. 'How can you simply wallow in your own cosy set-up while others out there fight your wars for you?'

But Caspar could.

He dropped the last rinsed plate into the drying rack. The fact was, Caspar thought, not for the first time, not for the last: the years between them simply were too long.

2

Physician, heal thyself

Barbara was as outraged as her brother by the estimate from the Partridge.

'It can't cost this much!' she gasped. 'That's absolutely ridiculous. There must be some mistake.' She ran a finger down the thick cream paper studded with wedding words: flowers, champagne, table settings, cake . . .

'Have you checked the figures?' she asked William, still aghast, waving it under his nose. But it was Miguel-Angel who prised the flapping sheet from between her fingers. Tipping his head back, he inspected it.

'Is it good?'

'Good?' William said sourly. 'It's positively *princely*.'

Caspar gave him a warning frown.

'It's fine,' he soothed, and Miguel-Angel shrugged. Snatching the sheet of paper back, Barbara waved it at Caspar.

'No, it's not. We can't go on with this. I'd no idea!'

'Nonsense, Barbara. It's all booked.'

Still, he could not resist letting his eye be caught again by the extraordinary final figure that stood out in bolder, even more frightening, type. It wasn't anything to wipe out a man of means. It probably wasn't even anything outrageous in the world's estimation. But it was certainly a hefty enough dollop of loot to focus the mind on the meaning and value of marriage, both as an institution and in the particular case. Caspar could not exactly give

Barbara and Miguel-Angel the once-over and ask himself, are the two of them worth it? But he could try and banish the vision of a lost luxurious holiday, a large lump-sum pension payment, maybe even one or two nice prints, by telling himself that Barbara was, after all, a whole lot less of an eyesore than the last time he saw her. Three weeks of fizzy water had done its whack to rid her of that awful bloated look. She was almost halfway to becoming attractive. And a good thing too. Any bride who cost this much ought to be bloody brilliant.

'You're looking very well.'

'Too busy to overeat,' she said proudly. 'Weightwatchers on Monday, Dressmaker on Tuesday, Spanish lessons on Wednesday, Instruction on Thursday –'

William's face was a picture.

'*Religious* instruction?'

The sheer speed and efficacy of Miguel-Angel's intercession was the best testimony possible to the virtues of Catholic training. Instantly, he was on his feet.

'And Fridays we dance!'

He held out a hand to Barbara. Willingly, she rose. It was only a twirl or two. (Miguel-Angel obviously didn't approve of full-blooded showing off.) But it was graceful. The floor didn't shudder and the windows didn't shake. All his life, Caspar had heard the same kind-hearted tosh as everyone else about fat people being graceful on their toes and, frankly, never believed a word of it. Some of the barrage balloons he'd had his arm up or his laparoscope inside would be hard-pressed, he reckoned, to billow their way in and out of the Ladies without causing structural damage. But here was Barbara, proving him wrong.

Graciously, Miguel-Angel handed her back to her chair.

'And how is everything at Cold Domain?' asked Caspar, making an equally gracious attempt to let Miguel-Angel know that his distraction had bipartisan support. The man had been over the threshold fewer than five minutes; but from his very first gesture (lifting a finger to his upper lip and drooping it artfully into a moustache shape while he winked at Caspar over Barbara's head) Caspar had formed the view that here at last was a dependable ally against the emotional excesses of the Collett tribe. He handed Miguel-Angel his sherry and Barbara her soda water. 'Everyone well?' he persisted.

'I don't know,' Barbara said cheerfully. 'I haven't been back for weeks. Not since the giant row.'

Sensing their bewilderment, she lifted her nose from the deliciously exploding bubbles.

'Surely you heard?'

'Heard what?' demanded William.

Barbara blushed.

'After you two drove off, Mother and I had a little bit of a spat.'

'You quarrelled with *Mother*?'

Barbara nodded, adding as a proud afterthought:

'And Tory. And Gillyflower.'

'And you haven't seen any of them *since*?'

'I've been waiting for their apologies,' Barbara said lightly.

'For three whole *weeks*?' He turned to Caspar with a histrionic gesture that caused Miguel-Angel to raise a disapproving eyebrow. 'Three weeks she's not talking to the other wedding guests, and she doesn't even bother to tell me!'

Belatedly, he recalled who was paying the piper.

'Or you,' he added hastily.

Glancing a little warily at Miguel-Angel, Barbara made an effort to account for her lapse.

'I did mean to phone you, William. In fact, I'm sure I tried a couple of times straight after the stupid business happened. But you two weren't back yet.' She waved her chubby little hands about to try and mask the fact that her explanation was already running out of steam. 'And then . . .' She shrugged. 'Oh, you know . . .'

'No. I don't know.'

And Caspar didn't either. He gazed at Barbara with an astonishment equal to William's, then turned to Miguel-Angel; but there was something in that impassive, chiselled face that gave the onlooker to understand that he was not prepared to lower himself even to be a part of this conversation, let alone try and offer enlightenment. Even as Caspar watched, he picked up one of the medical journals that Caspar had only at the last moment remembered to substitute for the provocative mix of 'special interest' magazines that William still made a point of leaving round the flat, and disappeared behind it.

Caspar turned back to Barbara. But she, clearly impatient to leave the whole topic behind her, was now rather obviously directing her attention to the room's careful decoration and furnishings. What mystified Caspar most was the extraordinary change wrought in this woman over the last three weeks. Where was the cringing, sobbing blob who used to telephone her brother night after night to chew for hours over some petty Mrs Collett cruelty? Gone. Vanished. And in her place sat this serene matron who, offered the option of the usual overwrought inquest into what might prove, in the circumstances of the approaching wedding, to be a critical family estrangement, clearly preferred a covert inspection of the quality of his floor rugs and the style of ruffle on top of his curtains. All this was obviously Miguel-Angel's influence. Even after such a short time, Caspar could see the man was capable of transmitting an almost incandescent emotional indifference into the atmosphere around him. But how had he managed to prevail upon Barbara? Were all his pockets filled with magic dust? Did he have wands to wave?

Or wands to spare? For, as he sat watching this astonishingly self-possessed foreigner leaf tranquilly through page after unintelligible page about sutures and transplants and mesenteric adhesions, it came to Caspar suddenly, with a pang, that the admiration he was feeling was riddled with envy. If only William could be as successfully dislodged from his obsession with his family, his worn old psychic tracks. Already he was harrying his sister for the details he craved.

'The quarrel, Barbara. What about the *quarrel*?'

Without thinking, Barbara reached for the packet of cigarettes Caspar had left on the coffee table. Just as he realized he hadn't yet seen her smoking on this visit, she drew one out. She'd raised it almost to her lips before Miguel-Angel slid out from behind his medical journal like the moon from between clouds, and prised it out of her fingers. Caspar expected him to push it neatly back inside the packet. But no. Without a word, he snapped the cigarette in two, and ground the splayed halves in the ashtray before going calmly back to his magazine.

Well, that was one way to stop her smoking other people's. Caspar was awestruck. His growing sense of wonder at Miguel-Angel's powers quite distracted him as, under William's fierce prompting, Barbara's determination finally weakened, and she came out, piecemeal and practically back to front, with an extraordinary tale in which, insofar as Caspar successfully followed it, Mrs Collett's less than lukewarm cooperation in meeting the groom ('I'm afraid next week is a little bit busy') had driven Barbara once too often through humiliation to bursting point. And when her mother had the nerve to round off a series of rebuffed opportunities with a pleasantry of almost psychopathic hypocrisy ('Well, dear, I very much hope I'll get the chance to meet him soon'), the worm that was Barbara had apparently turned.

'Don't get too excited,' I told her. 'At this rate, you may have a long wait.'

Caspar watched William lean forward, the better to drink in the details of this exhilarating battle.

'What did she *say*?'

Barbara shrugged.

'Nothing. She just put on that steel-trap face of hers. Gilly tried peace-making at once, of course, acting stupid to give me a chance to change my mind and step back from the precipice.'

'What did *she* say?'

Barbara's mantle of indifference cracked.

'Would you *believe*? She said, "Why? Are you having a long engagement?"'

William burst out laughing. 'Oh, well tried, Gillyflower!' He leaned even closer, till he was practically off his chair in his excitement. 'But you kept blundering on?'

'I certainly did. I told everyone, "No. We're not having a long engagement. Mother's just going to have a long wait. If she can't even be bothered to meet Miguel-Angel

78

now, when he works right next door, she's certainly not going to meet him at the wedding. Because she bloody well won't be invited!"'

William's face shone with joy. Caspar had rarely seen him so ecstatic.

'I bet she didn't stay long after that!'

'On her feet in a flash. But I wasn't much slower. I got to the door before Tory and Gilly, and stopped them getting out after her.' Hugging herself with a pleasure that matched William's, she failed to notice Miguel-Angel's lowered journal, or his stern look. Caught up at last in the excitement of telling the story, she went on delightedly, 'I tell you, the two of them looked absolutely terrified, as if I was some fat witch explaining the curse I'd put on the family. "It's no use you staring at me as if I'm mad," I told them. "I've simply had enough. I've never asked her for anything in my whole life. Not anything. Not till now. When I think of all the things I've done for her over the last few years, and she's just sat there, hardly ever even bothering to say thank you properly. Well, she can just think again. And so can you two. I *mean* it. You can go chasing down the garden after her a thousand times. But if she's too mean to let me get married here, if she can't even be bothered to meet the man I love, then she bloody well can't come to the wedding. And if you won't support me, then you can't come either!"'

'My God!' said William. 'Did you say all that?'

'I certainly did,' said Barbara. 'And they deserved it.'

In sheer jubilation, William hugged his sister. His face was radiant, his happiness complete. Cold Domain 2 – Rest of the World 0, Caspar thought bitterly, recalling

Barbara's tearful revelation on the stairs that everything unconnected to her childhood stamping ground seemed little more than shadow life. She could have been speaking for her brother too, he realized suddenly. In this respect at least, they might be twins. For all his efforts over five long years, when had he ever managed to put a light like that in William's eyes, or hold his attention so raptly?

'So what did *Tory* say?'

'Oh, she was furious. And Gilly –'

'Barbara! Enough!'

The stern look might have stayed unnoticed above the journal. The stern voice hit the spot. Instantly, Barbara could not have shown herself more penitent.

'I'm sorry, Miguel-Angel! I really didn't mean to go on about it. I forgot.'

William was outraged.

'Excuse me,' he said icily to his prospective brother-in-law. 'But Barbara and I happen to be halfway through a conversation.'

'No,' Miguel-Angel corrected him. 'Barbara has finished.'

The glorious Spaniard calmly returned to his magazine.

William spun round on Barbara.

'Are you taking this?'

Caspar watched Barbara take the deepest breath.

'Yes,' she said. 'Yes, I am. I'm taking it because I think he's right. You and I just go on and on about everything to do with Cold Domain. It's a bad habit and there isn't any point. We're not children any longer, and I'm stopping.'

She spread her hands.

'It's like the cigarettes,' she said. 'I'm giving it up.'

'The man says jump, and you jump?'

'No,' she said firmly. 'I've listened to what he has to say and, after careful thought, I find I agree with him.'

Caspar stepped forward. William's look was mean. But William shook him off.

'So what *does* Miguel-Angel say?'

Dropping the journal to the floor, the man under discussion rose to his feet.

'I say,' he said slowly and carefully, 'a family like this is not a family.' He held out his hand to Barbara, and obediently she rose to stand at his side. 'I say that Barbara is now for me, not for her mother and not for her sisters. I say the past is over and the future begins.'

In the silence that followed, Caspar sank on the arm of the nearest chair. Barbara was beside him in an instant. Totally misinterpreting his moment of weakness, she rushed into a flurry of apologies.

'Oh, Caspar! You've been so generous, and now we're all squabbling under your roof. I'm so sorry!'

He shook his head. 'Don't be silly, Barbara.' He patted her hand. How could he possibly explain that it was not the argument that made the floor shake, the walls rock, the very air round him shiver. It was this paragon of quiet purpose. It was Miguel-Angel. A man like this should marry like a prince. In his mind's eye, Caspar could already see him standing waiting at the altar – a little stiffly, sternly almost, dressed in the purest white – for he was a hero; dauntless; a very god. Caspar was dizzy, yes. And dizzy with desire. But not for the Spaniard's firm body, nor for his strength, nor for his matchless virtue. What made Caspar's flesh tremble and his head swirl was the deep and unquenchable longing that swept without warning over this, the most cautious of doctors, the most prudent of citizens, to pay for the man's wedding though it cost the earth.

Cost the earth . . . Oh, God! Caspar could scarcely hear Barbara's murmurs of concern for the crowing of cocks in his ears. Making the most tremendous effort, he eased himself out of her protective embrace, and tried to pull himself together.

'Really, it's nothing. Just for a moment I felt giddy, that's all.'

'All this fuss!' Barbara insisted. 'It's too much for anyone.'

He nodded agreement, even as, through the striae of his fractured vision, he had a preview of far greater fuss to come. Astonishing that the shit had still not hit the fan. Part of the explanation, of course, must lie in Barbara's extraordinary series of revelations. If she was out every night, practising dancing and starving and praying, and trying on frocks, then she wasn't in the unit to pick up the telephone. So Mrs Collett's planning application could be making its way (possibly in triplicate) through the sort of slack rural council where everyone had known everyone else ever since nursery school, and married one another's cousins, and still the news had yet to filter back. Three weeks ago, Caspar had reckoned on a few days' grace at most before some old school chum of Barbara's was on the phone: 'I hear from a friend in Land Registry that your mother's finally selling off that lovely old garden,' or some soil-stained old codger flagged down her car as she slowed for the gates, to stake his scavenging claims: 'You might mention to your mother, if she's looking for a good home for that dwarf japonica before the bulldozers get it . . .'

But Barbara hadn't been back. She didn't know. The bulldozers were practically through the gate, and only Caspar and Mrs Collett, twinned (quite unwittingly on her part) in conspiracy, knew anything about it. Through Caspar's guilty brain ground the noise of giant mechanical teeth taking their first juddering bite of earth. He saw root balls rip apart, and rose bushes tumble, broken-backed, down muddy slopes studded with shattered fruit trees and pulped blossom. Catching his breath, he plucked his shirt away from his chest, suddenly awash with fear.

'Are you all right, Caspar? You look very pale.'

'I'm fine. I'm fine.'

Shoulders down, breathe out slowly, take your time . . . Physician, heal thyself.

'Really, I'm fine.'

3
'*Give me the moonlight . . .*'

Caspar lay on his back on the damp grass and gazed up through the silvered branches of the sycamore.

'*Give me the moonlight,*' he sang softly, waving hands almost blue under the milky sheen that poured down so generously. '*Give me the girl. And leave the –*'

'Ssh!' William told him.

'Ssh! yourself.'

'Ssh!' William said again. 'I'm *thinking.*'

There'd been enough occasions on which Caspar the off-duty gynaecologist had been expected to make decisions about life and death with William talking in his other ear. But, as he knew, only a fool assumed that partnership meant equal rights. So he obediently switched off the voice, and hummed the song in his brain. Why spoil a beautiful night? And it was beautiful. More beautiful than any he could remember. The moon was glorious. She hung so huge. She spilled such light. She overflowed with magic. The tree above him was extraordinary. A vaulted masterpiece. Look at the branches! The grandeur of their uplifted arms, the glory of their tracery.

'Maybe there *is* a God . . .'

'Ssh!'

And all the shadows round. Some cool substantial shapes, some spectrally intriguing, some nothing more than fleeting impressions of a deeper dark.

'We ought to live outside, you know. Outside at night.'

'Be *quiet*, Caspar!'

But why? After all, it wasn't as if anyone would hear him. What time was it? Four in the morning. The last dark hour, when even Mrs Collett must be sleeping.

'Right,' William said. 'I think I've got it.'

You had to hand it to him if he had. From what Caspar overheard of Barbara's instructions, this raid was Mission Impossible. 'It's still exactly where it was,' she'd told her brother. 'In that old biscuit tin buried next to the flagstone walk.'

'The one she took up last year?'

'No, silly. The one she took up years ago, when she got rid of the cold frames.'

'The one that ran down the side of the box hedge?'

'What box hedge?'

'You must remember the box hedge. It went all the way from where the laburnum used to be to where she ripped out that acacia.'

'Oh, yes.' Her look of mystification cleared. 'It's been gone so long I'd forgotten. Yes. That's the path. Well, you go down where that walk used to be —'

'Past that lovely old wooden bench.'

'Lovely old wooden bench?'

'Well, not any *longer*, obviously,' snapped William.

'Oh, yes. Well. Past where that lovely old wooden bench was, and then, right next to where that flowering cherry used to be, you should find a bit of a slope from where the steps were —'

'Unless she's had a go at the slope.'

'That's possible. I haven't had a good scout round recently. But you shouldn't miss it. The tin was about a foot to the left of the third flagstone from the sundial.'

'Sundial?' said Caspar, before thinking better of it.

Together, they turned to glare.

'Sorry,' said Caspar.

'Anyway,' Barbara told her brother, 'it's there. Do you think you'll be able to find it?'

'Oh, yes,' said William with total confidence. 'I'm sure I'll be able to find it.'

'Don't bring the whole tin back,' said Barbara. 'I like to think of it still buried there. Just bring the blue glass beads.'

'The blue glass beads. Rely on me.'

So here they were, at dead of night, except you couldn't call this garden dead. It seemed to be living, breathing, sentient. A world of its own, out of time, watching them trespass and listening to William's muttered fretting.

'I don't get this at all. The pear tree can't have moved. The old greenhouse was there, that's obvious. You can still see bits of its brick base. And the wall must be in the same place, for God's sake . . .'

'Well done, wall!'

'Shh!' William gazed round in misery. 'So where the hell was the box hedge? I can't work it out at all. Too much has gone.'

He dropped to his knees beside Caspar.

'It used to be all cramped and secret round here,' he said. 'Little holes. Little hiding places. Little tracks. Things to peep over. Places to hide.' He spread his hands in the moonlight. 'Now look at it. It's like the bloody *steppes*. There's nothing here. Nothing but flat bloody grass!'

Sensing the rising panic, Caspar moved fast. On his knees in an instant, he took William's trembling hands in his.

'Shut your eyes. Breathe out slowly. Shoulders down.'

William made a face, but did what he was told. Slowly his pulse settled under Caspar's expert thumb. Caspar surveyed his options. He could take William on, or take him back. Better to take him back. But then they would have to face Barbara without the contents of the biscuit tin. And she had set her heart on those glass beads. 'Something old, something new, something borrowed, something blue.' Really, the way these female mysteries chewed up the hours, it was small wonder so few women reached the top in their chosen professions.

Better go on. And Caspar had no doubt William could manage it. If Caspar's patients could rise over pain (and, sometimes, agony) then William could triumph over memory. As the myriad broken nights testified, it was all in there somewhere.

'Keep your eyes shut.'

Caspar raised William to his feet, and turned him round to face the one fixed lodestar, the immovable wall.

'Open your eyes.'

William opened them with a deliberate flutter. At once the thought came to Caspar that this was probably the only opportunity he'd ever get to violate (at a stroke, as it were) both Mrs Collett's son and Mrs Collett's garden. But the timing of the offer irritated him so mightily that he resolutely chose to ignore it.

'Look at the wall. Got it? Now shut your eyes again, and keep them shut. Relax. Think yourself back. Go back. Right back. You're nine years old. You're outside in the dark. You've seen the wall. You know exactly where you are. You know this garden – every leaf of it. You don't need any help. You know the way.'

He let go of William and waited. Off William went,

moving quite calmly over the dark grass, past all the things that were no longer there, running his fingers over the lovely old wooden bench (or maybe the flowering cherry, it wasn't clear). He stepped across the lawn with perfect confidence, taking a step to the left here, a wide curve there, like one of those birds Caspar had read about who still, after thousands of years, made detours in flight in order to avoid some hazard gone in all but memory. Once or twice he walked oddly, and Caspar realized that he was going up (or down) little imaginary steps.

And then he turned. Placing his heel back firmly against a sundial that wasn't there, he paced out three flagstones whose size and shape was vivid in his memory.

'Here,' he said, pointing about a foot to the left.

Caspar picked up the trowel.

'Well done. You can open your eyes now.'

While William watched, his eyes gleaming in the half dark, Caspar stabbed at the grass. The smell of earth released by the first few trowelfuls set off a momentary rush of sympathy for William's aching love. This *was* the real world, thought Caspar. William was right. Even the lovely clean gases and chemicals and disinfectants of the hospital could not compare with this cold, dank, elemental odour. This was the base of things. This was the source.

'Anything?'

'Not yet.'

And then the trowel struck home.

'Go easy! No need to stove the bloody thing in.'

'Do you want to do it yourself?'

'Just be *careful*.'

Caspar was careful. No doubt the hospital took every precaution to make sure all his shots were up to date. But one should never tempt Providence. Why *invite* tetanus? Why *welcome* septicaemia? He used the side of the trowel to brush the loose earth from the top of the tin, and lever off the badly rusted lid.

He struck a match.

'Jeepers! What *is* all this?'

William wormed himself over the grass sufficiently close to peer in when the next match flared.

'Oh, look! Farthings! And threepenny bits! Bab's old lucky bone. And Fortune's collar.' He poked at a desic-cated and misshapen lump. 'What's this? Oh, never mind. There's the beads, anyway.'

'These?'

Caspar fished them out.

'Never beads,' he said. 'They're just rubbishy old stones.'

'Nonsense.'

Caspar rolled them over his palm.

'Or bits of old tile, or something.'

'What does it matter, if they're what she wants?'

And Caspar couldn't say. But all the time that he was stamping down the earth, and putting the trowel back, and following William across the lawn and through what was left of the shrubbery, he couldn't help letting the small, rebellious thought burgeon and grow. Of course it mattered. To drive from London in the middle of the night to dig up a handful of buried glass beads was, as daft ideas went, just about thinkable. (Well, after all, they'd done it.) But if he had known they were going to turn out to be nothing more than a few worthless chippings of something a pretty blue colour, he would never have bothered. It was as simple as that. Old glass was one thing, and pitted lumps of broken tile were quite another. Barbara had been entirely tricked by memory. The treasure she craved was so much dug-up rubbish. And just suppose that exactly the same sort of sleight of mind had taken place in William? Caspar spun round to take a last look at the moonlit garden and see it how it was, razed to the walls and spirit-level flat, bereft of interest, stripped of ornament. Forget William's fancy trippings and curlicues around imagined old glories. Who was to say it hadn't always been a fairly mundane place?

Another reason to be rid of the whole bloody cabbage patch.

4

Heart of butter, heart of steel

After a day's anguished nail-biting, William phoned Tory.

'I really would prefer not to get involved in this, William,' she said in her pickle-up-the-arse voice.

William hung up on her, and instantly, before she could get on the line first and thwart him, punched Gilly-flower's number.

'Not sure she's in,' said Angus warily.

'Of course she's in,' snapped William. 'It's half past ten. I want to talk to her, Angus.'

He drummed his fingers on the telephone till Angus came back.

'She's in the bath. She'll phone you tomorrow.'

'I want her *now*.'

Angus hung up.

William phoned Barbara's unit, and hung on, interminably, while someone who clearly had no idea at all who Barbara was found someone else who said she wasn't there.

'Why are you bothering with all this?' Caspar asked, putting a whisky and soda down beside the telephone.

To save himself from having to say thank you for the drink, William ignored it.

'There's something fishy going on,' he said for the twentieth time. 'She's up to something, my mother. I can tell.'

Caspar turned away, pretending to need something

from the kitchen. Could William smell collusion? Did guilt show?

'Nothing makes sense,' said William. 'Look at the facts. She has a giant row with Barbara. The worst row ever. It goes on for *weeks*. And yet you saw the garden yesterday. Nothing's changed. Nothing's gone.'

'You said yourself that it was like the bloody steppes.'

William dismissed the reminder with a petulant gesture.

'Nothing new. Nothing since last time. And she's had three whole weeks! Three weeks to brood and fret, and think poisonous thoughts about her eldest daughter getting married only next door, over the wall, within *earshot*, for God's sake, and her not even invited. There must be people running up to her in the street by now. "I hear Barbara's finally about to tie the knot. How splendid for you all. Weddings are so *exciting*."' He waggled his head from side to side. '"What? Not *invited*? Lilith, *dear*!"'

Dropping the mimicry, he banged his fist against the bookshelf.

'She must be *steaming* with rage. Why's nothing *gone*?'

Guilt made Caspar stupid.

'Nothing left to go?'

'Don't be ridiculous,' snapped William. 'There's always something left to go. We've learned that over the years.' Narrowing his eyes, he ran a memory check over the garden they'd strolled through the night before. 'There wasn't anything,' he said. 'Nothing that wasn't gone before. I didn't see any raw tree stumps. There weren't any suspicious hollows in the ground. No freshly stripped patches of wall. And what's really worrying is that there were no signs of her trying anything, either. No cans of Tumbleweed beside the dustbin. No axe left near the fruit trees. There wasn't even much fresh greenery on the compost heap.'

He turned to Caspar.

'What could be going on? What is she planning?'

Planning. The very word made Caspar shudder. But add one more, and say them both out loud, and he'd be free again. Just say it. 'Planning permission.' And bring this great juggernaut of guilt and shame juddering to a firm halt. See off the cocks that crowed. Unable to bear the weight of the secret a single moment longer, Caspar took a deep breath. Begging his set face to give nothing – nothing at all – away, he offered blandly:

'Maybe your mother's stopped bothering with the garden because –'

The hesitation, though momentary, was enough to tip crosspatch William over the edge.

'Because *what*?' he snapped. 'Because she's too upset to pick up her saw? Too livid to oil her secateurs? Too outraged to slot a refill in her weedkiller syringe?'

His sheer unpleasantness reminded Caspar of just what it was about this obsession that had set him on this track in the first place. His heart of butter turned right back to steel.

'Because she's too ill?' he ventured instead.

William almost spat.

'Ill!'

'She *might* be . . .'

'And stones might catch pneumonia! She's never ill.'

But the moment had passed, and Caspar couldn't care less now.

'Maybe she's gone away,' he offered indifferently.

'Gone away?'

93

Somehow William managed to make it sound as if the words he was echoing came from some language that he didn't know.

'Everyone goes away sometimes.'

'My mother doesn't.'

Caspar said, exasperated,

'Then maybe she's *dead*.'

This, he couldn't help noticing, was the first idea to which William appeared willing to attach any credence.

'She might be dead,' he admitted. 'Lying in the house, electrocuted by mistake, or something. Or maybe even murdered for her jewellery.'

'Not if it's no better than Barbara's,' Caspar said, fingering the tiny square lumps in his pocket. (He still resented the loss of most of a night's sleep and half a tank of petrol.) But William wasn't listening. Shaking his head, he was regretfully tossing the idea of his mother's death out of court.

'No,' he said. 'She can't be. I'd have heard by now. Tory or Gillyflower would have told me.'

But still, the notion had done its bit to cheer him up. Though it didn't distract him from grim supposition. Snatching up the whisky Caspar had once again slid within reach (once again without thanking him), he was soon off again.

'No. There is something fishy going on. My mother's up to something. But what? What? *What*?'

5

And with whom?

And with whom? Was Tory in on this? Was Gillyflower? Shamelessly, Caspar traded two sneaky telephone calls against one infertility clinic. Broadbent was thrilled.

'All I have to do is phone these two numbers?'

'That's right.'

'And see where I get with these questions?'

'Yes.'

'That's it? And you do the whole of tonight's clinic? It's a deal!'

They ousted Sister Fairway to use the only telephone on which Caspar could comfortably listen in. Broadbent threw himself into the part with the zeal of the broker who knows himself grossly overcompensated for his efforts.

'Is that Mrs McFarlane?'

'That's right,' said Gillyflower, clearly in fright from the outset at the sound of a strange voice.

'Oh, good,' said Broadbent. 'Now, about this planning application on my desk —'

'What planning application?'

The mystification sounded genuine.

'Is it possible I have the wrong number?' said Broadbent. 'You're not acting as a back-up telephone number for your mother?'

'My *mother*?'

Caspar nodded at Broadbent, who promptly closed.

'This is Mrs *James Allan* McFarlane?'

Disproportionately relieved, Gilly's voice filled the freshly painted little cubicle. 'Oh, *there's* your mistake. My husband's name is Angus. We have nothing to do with any planning application.'

'So sorry to have troubled you,' Broadbent trilled. 'A stupid clerical error. Forget I called.'

He switched off the fancy phone.

'Happy?'

Caspar nodded.

'Then let's do the other one.'

But before he was halfway through the number, Caspar had laid a hand on his. If Tory knew, she'd have told Gillyflower. And Gilly didn't know. Why risk the two of them comparing notes? 'I had a very strange call today from a man at the council.' 'That's funny. So did I.' No. Better to leave it.

'You'll still do the whole clinic, won't you?' Already, Broadbent was struggling out of his white coat and into his jacket. 'If you're quite *ruthless*, you'll be home by nine.'

6

He was like me. I am like Hector.
William is like her

At five to ten, Nurse dropped the very last of the brown folders on the desk in front of Caspar.

'Miss Barbara Collett.'

'Good God Almighty!'

And Barbara, sailing through the door, was equally put out.

'Oh, Caspar! This is too bad! I made a point of checking that it wouldn't be you.' She fished her appointment card out of her handbag. 'I'm supposed to have someone called Broadhurst.'

'Broadbent,' corrected Caspar, trying to gather his wits. He glanced down at the folder in front of him. 'I can't understand how you can have been referred here anyhow,' he said, just before catching sight of his very own home address, flat number and all, typed on the label underneath her name.

'Oh, really!' he burst out. But Nurse was standing there with ears on stalks. It was clearly not the moment to pursue it.

Barbara peeled off the gloves she'd taken to wearing to protect her nails.

'You always said this was the best place.'

'Depends on your problem,' Caspar said warily. The fear was growing in him that Barbara's evident desire for professional advice would, any moment now, outweigh her initial antipathy to the idea of his providing it. Steepling his fingers to raise a further barrier between them, he

97

made his own position clear. 'I realize you've come a long way. And whatever the problem turns out to be, I'd be delighted to give you any advice I can. But, frankly, I don't think I ought to be the one to examine you. Possibly you'd regret it later. So let me just put you straight down for another appointment.'

In Barbara, frustration fought visibly with common sense.

'Won't it take *weeks* again?'

'Not if I fiddle things about a bit.'

Sensing the rustle of disapproval at his side, he swivelled in the chair. 'I shan't be examining Miss Collett,' he said firmly. 'So if you'd like to see about finishing up . . .'

Sullenly, the nurse began gathering her boxes and files. Caspar filled the silence by scrabbling under one side of his white coat and digging in his trouser pocket.

'Since you're here, Barbara . . .'

He pushed them across the desk towards her.

'My blue glass beads!' She shrieked with glee. 'Oh, Caspar! You *found* them!'

'They're never glass,' he said firmly, determined to distract her from mentioning William until the nurse was safely out of the room. 'They look like scruffy old bits of tile to me.'

Barbara scooped them protectively into her palm.

'You're wrong. They're made of a very, very old sort of glass.'

The nurse was almost at the door now.

'And if they're supposed to be beads,' Caspar persisted, 'Why don't they have any thread holes?'

Barbara wriggled on her seat in defeat.

'All right,' she admitted, just as the nurse finally closed

the door behind her. 'You and William can laugh at me for calling them beads. They're actually bits of mosaic.'

'Mosaic?'

'Ancient Roman mosaic. Out of the garden.'

'You had a Roman mosaic at Cold Domain?'

He held out his hand, and Barbara obediently dropped one of the little blue square lumps back in his palm. While he inspected it properly for the first time, she told him cheerfully:

'It must be one of the few things that's still there.' Her smile widened. 'Unless she's been so livid these last weeks that she's dug the whole boiling up. But I doubt it. Out of sight, out of mind, and it is three feet down. Tory and I found it after the foundations for the garage were dug, and we decided to keep going to Australia.'

'But wasn't there a great fuss?' Caspar tipped the little blue fragment across the palm of his hand. What he'd taken in the moonlight for a poorly fired surface now looked like the patina of age. What in his irritation he'd thought worthless now looked curiously timeless and beautiful. He glanced up. 'Surely you must have had hordes of archaeologists insisting you stopped building the garage, and men from the ministry trying to turn you into a site of historical interest?'

'They never knew anything about it.'

'How come?'

Barbara blushed.

'Well, even from the little bit Tory and I scraped clear, you could tell it was rude . . .'

'Rude?'

The blush deepened, till Caspar couldn't help but wonder what colour she'd have gone if he'd examined her.

'You know. People doing things. I expect it was part of some sort of bath-house, but even so . . .' Her voice trailed away as she relived her twelve-year-old disgust. 'Anyway,' she finished up, 'as soon as Mother saw it, that was it. She made my father fill the hole in at once. She said she wasn't going to have perfect strangers nosing around in her garden, and especially not for something like that. They could all wait another hundred years, till she was safely dead and gone, and someone else lived there.'

'And Hector didn't argue?'

'He might have put up a bit of a fight, I suppose. But I doubt it. He'd started on his precious garage, after all. And he must have known how much he'd suffer if she didn't get her way.'

He was like me, thought Caspar in a wave of gloom. I am like Hector. William is like her.

'So she told us to throw every last chip of it back, and it was filled in again.' Almost with difficulty she opened the hand in which she'd kept the fragments of mosaic tightly clutched through the story. 'I stole these. Maybe they became so precious to me just because I had to keep them so secret. It was quite an issue. We were forbidden ever to speak of it to anyone.'

'I must say William's never mentioned it to me.'

'William? I doubt if William's ever given it a thought. He can't have been much more than a toddler when it happened.'

She started gathering her things to leave. Nodding at the file on the desk between them, she said to Caspar,

'You promise me you won't read that?'

'I promise,' Caspar said. 'And I promise I'll get you another appointment in no time.'

She tipped the bits of mosaic into her glove for safety.

'And you won't tell William I came?'

'Then you had better give me back your lucky beads.'

'They're not *lucky*,' she couldn't help correcting him as she tipped them back into his hand. 'Though, now I think about it, I did once have a lucky bone.'

For fear of the loss of more sleep and more petrol, Caspar forbore to mention it was found.

He dropped one little dusky blue lump back in her glove – just in case.

'I'll post the rest to you. At your *real* address . . .'

She had the grace to look penitent. And, for that moment, she looked beautiful. He was still staring after her when she reached the door.

'Caspar,' she said, turning back to him. 'I've never told you this. I've been embarrassed. But I'm glad you're with William. I think you're good for him. I think I trust you always to know exactly what he needs.'

Then, even more embarrassed, she turned and fled. As soon as he was sure the click of her fancy new high heels was fading along the corridor, he pulled the thin sheaf of notes out of her file and settled down to read. But there was nothing to them. Barbara's own doctor's internal examination had come up with nothing abnormal. As far as Caspar could make out, Barbara's great gynaecological predicament consisted of little more than a conviction that she must be infertile because two protracted affairs had left her cradling no infants. Naturally, the file was dumb on whether the men concerned had reasonable sperm counts. Or whether either relationship, while it lasted, had been conducive to fertility. (Caspar had more than once suggested a husband reschedule his two week-

ends home a month with impressive procreative results.)
Nothing was known about the two men at all. Indeed,
Caspar himself was well ahead of Barbara's case notes in
the research stakes. He at least knew from idle eavesdrop-
ping that one of the fellows concerned used to work in a
garage, and the other was always referred to as 'that
awful bossy Bernard'. For God's sake! Broadbent was
going to have a hard time taking this one seriously. How
Barbara had even managed to get a referral to a specialist
was beyond him.

Probably forged it, along with his address. What a
family!

But a promise is a promise. Sighing, Caspar slid an
envelope and a sheet of paper out of the tray at his side.
After a moment's thought, he wrote: *To J. Broadbent
[Confidential]* on the envelope. And then, inside:

Dear Jim,
Could you possibly do me another small favour . . .?

7

'Tessera, tesserae'

He woke in the middle of the night, convinced he was screaming his head off. The bloody bulldozer was back. But this time the earth it tore apart glittered with ancient fragments in water blues and water greens and water greys. The lovely mosaic paving reared up and shattered in the air as Roman men were wrenched from Roman women, arms ripped from shoulder sockets, breasts split, thighs exploded, and tiny fragments like Barbara's flew through the air.

'*Tessera, tesserae*,' he found himself murmuring, though he'd have sworn that all his Latin left him thirty years ago.

Beside him, a crooked elbow and a spill of hair lay between dislodged pillows. The barest graze of breathing came from a mound that scarcely rose and fell.

William, the usual fracturer of nights, was sleeping like a baby.

8

Ready and waiting

Stepping out of her car in the usual flurry of embarrassment, Barbara failed to notice the two men from the
council tautening a measuring tape between them, from
the veranda to the Partridge's side wall. She hurried
through the service door, and took the uncarpeted back
stairs up to Miguel-Angel's tiny room. As usual, the door
swung open before she even had time to knock.

He took her raised hand in his, and kissed it.

'*Bar-bar-a!*'

The way he said it made it sound as plosive as a swear
word. ('*Bar-bar-ous!*' mimicked William, complaining that
every time he heard Miguel-Angel come out with his
sister's name, he was beset by visions of hordes of stinking
ruffians swarming across the steppes.) But Barbara
couldn't bring herself to say a word about it to her
beloved. She prized him so highly that everything he did
or said was lit by her love and warmed by her devotion.

'I thought I might be late.'

He lifted his hands in mock horror.

'No clocks in here.'

He took her coat, and hung it to cover his dressing-
gown on the back of the door. She was about to sink, as
usual, on to the faded candlewick bedspread when, lightly
but firmly, he handed her into the room's only chair
before turning the glossy back of his waistcoat to stare out
of the window while she gingerly lowered herself into it.

The rush of colour to her face took its time to subside. She didn't know which embarrassed her more: realizing he'd guessed she always took the bed for fear of getting stuck between the narrow chair arms, or knowing he could appraise her body with such accuracy, he knew the day it would be safe to try.

'Good week?' he asked, turning back to smile at the pride and delight that had supplanted her blushes.

'Lovely,' she said, settling back carefully against the thin cushion. 'Those wheelchair parts came, and that made things a whole lot easier. And Ellie's ex-husband mended the bath harness. And Bunster and Dido made up again.'

'Made up?'

He pointed to his face, and raised an eyebrow. Did he realize how beautiful he was? Oh, how had he ever stepped, so unimagined, so unlooked for, into her drab little life? She owed him everything, and longed for him so much she felt a stab of pain. In the end he was forced to repeat himself, in order to prompt her out of her distraction.

'Made up?'

'Stopped quarrelling.'

'Ah. Quarrelling.' That glorious smile again. 'The national habit.'

She put out her hand, and, coming close, he dropped to his knees in front of her, burying his head in her lap as she dug her fingers into his hair. When he lifted his face for her kisses, she was ready and waiting, but she couldn't help trying to count them, such was her fear that one day this angel of a man would wake and find he'd changed his mind, and no longer wanted her. She knew enough about his kindness and courtesy to know he would let her down gently. Not like Andrew Taylor, who just blurted it out one morning while struggling with somebody's rusty bonnet catch. Or that horrible Bernard. No. Miguel-Angel's withdrawal would be careful. He'd take his time. And probably the only way she'd know would be that, one day, instead of being blessed with forty of his kisses, there'd be four.

'Enough. Enough.'

'Oh, please don't let's stop.'

'Barbara . . .' He slid her hand down to the rough serge bulge that proved how much he was suffering.

'I can fix that.'

'Barbara!' He kissed her warningly on the nose.

Pulling her dress straight, she made a face. But she no longer minded this strange conviction of his (strange, even for a Catholic) that only bad luck would come from breaking this one rule he'd set himself. She'd pointed out that she was no spring chicken. She'd even lied, and told him her doctor had agreed with her that every month counted at her age, and she'd be well advised to jump the gun. But Miguel-Angel was adamant. It was as if he really did believe that, like sin or crime, sex before marriage might lead to punishment. The day she'd shown him round her unit, he'd been horrified. He'd hidden it well enough – better than most. But she'd been working there for far too long not to see through all revulsion's human disguises. So now when he pulled apart from her, she too backed off, even though, nervous and embarrassed as she was, her soul would have sung to have him touch her all over. After the wedding it would be all right. And he'd be confident that all their babies would be whole and beautiful like him, not cruelly sabotaged like the busily straining damaged creatures amongst whom she spent her working life. She knew only too well how the insidious whisper could force an entry: be good, and you'll be lucky. Instantly she would feel ashamed, knowing the superstition for what it was, a vile, painful nonsense. She was a rational woman, and she'd known many of her patients' families through years of self-sacrifice and out-right heroism. She of all people knew that virtue never did and never would preclude disaster. But Miguel-Angel was different. He was old-fashioned, and had been brought up by people who believed there was some purpose in the universe, some mechanism of justice. And so, for love of him, she could fall in with this one primitive, idiosyncratic fear. After all, as her own mother's response to the announcement of their engagement suggested, it was prob-ably in this sheer foreignness of his that all the explanation lay for why he hadn't found her quite physically repellent. She was probably exactly the same size as his mother.

Or maybe a little smaller now. Could his mother fit in this chair? She'd love to know. But, after being fat so long, the only ways she had of asking someone else's size were curiously oblique.

She nodded at the brightly stamped envelope on the dresser.

'Is that a letter from home?'

'From my father.'

'Did he send any photographs?'

'Photographs?'

He glanced up from the handbag through which he was rooting, as usual, like a child. She could understand the attraction. He seemed to have so few possessions of his own that, every time she visited, he ended up fiddling with all the silly things she carried round with her. And what she loved was that, for all his customary courtesy, this was a pastime for which he never even asked permission. She was astonished the first time he tipped the lot out on to the bedspread – the lipsticks, the tiny tub of sugar substitute, keys, tweezers, eyeshadows, and all the rest of the paraphernalia of nursing and womanhood. And then he rooted through with perfect trust, as though it never occurred to him that somewhere in this cheap little treasure trove he might come across a hidden ring, or another man's photo, or (as once fell from Bernard's wallet) the last contraceptive from a previously unseen pack of three. Miguel-Angel slid open her tampon holders, and rubbed blobs of foundation cream on to his hand before looking up to see if it was the same shade she was wearing. If anyone else had taken such a liberty, she would have been furious. But, with him, it just seemed another way of saying 'I want to know everything about you and I trust you absolutely'.

Now he was lifting something out.

'What's this?'

He was holding up the little blue lump of mosaic.

'Something blue,' she told him. 'It's for the wedding. It's traditional. "*Something old, something new, something borrowed, something blue.*"' She added ruefully, 'Frankly, the way I've been spending money on clothes, I think I'll be the only something old.'

He smiled. 'And I'm the something new. And the wedding is something borrowed from Caspar.'

He paused. She realized he was looking serious. Then he reached for the letter on the dresser. 'No photographs,' he said. 'Better than photographs. My father sends me a date. He and my mother are coming to the wedding.'

Leaning across, he lay his finger over her lips before she could say a word.

'So now we must invite your mother too.'

He took his finger away.

'No,' Barbara told him.

'Yes,' Miguel-Angel insisted.

'No,' Barbara said again.

'It's important,' Miguel-Angel explained. 'Important to my mother. It's the first question she will ask. "Where is the other mother?" ' Tossing the lump of mosaic up in the air, he grinned at her. 'Like something blue, it is traditional.'

'I can't,' said Barbara. 'I took a vow.'

He raised an eyebrow, but he didn't question her. And she couldn't bring herself to try and explain – though who better than a man who believed he could barter his sexual restraint against the health of his offspring to understand how she could have pledged a vow sworn in anger against all their future happiness?

'I can't,' she said again.

'Very well,' he said, unrattled and undaunted. 'Someone else. Caspar.'

'You can't ask Caspar! Caspar's done enough!'

'Who else?'

Who else, indeed? She couldn't bear to think of asking Tory. And Gillyflower would make a hash of it. William was useless, of course. He would just end up making everything worse.

Yes, it would have to be Caspar.

Her submission led naturally to kisses. Kiss after kiss.

Thirty-five, forty, fifty. Barbara lost count. And when the alarm clock he'd hidden in his dressing-gown began to ping, to warn of his coming shift, her mouth was stinging and her face so flushed that she fled down the back stairs and out of the Partridge without even noticing the plastic-coated, all-weather copy of the official notice of the planning application, affixed by order to the site concerned.

9
'*Me?*'

Caspar was horrified. '*Me?*'

'You.'

'Why me? You must be joking!'

But he could tell that they were serious. Why else would they have come all the way to London to see him, on the train, if not to refuse to take no for an answer.

'Can't you ask someone else?'

'Who else?'

And Caspar could see Miguel-Angel's point. He wouldn't wish asking this favour of Tory on his worst enemy. Gillyflower was hopeless. The best she would manage would be to relay inaccurately back a few tiresome and hurtful remarks from her mother. And as for William . . .

Oh, for heaven's sake!

'All right,' he said. 'I'll do it.'

Barbara flung her arms around him.

'Oh, Caspar! You're so good to us.'

He pulled his bow tie back in place.

'Just don't expect miracles,' he warned them. But it was obvious from the expressions on their faces that both of them did. In Miguel-Angel's case, he put it down to being foreign, and in Barbara's to the unhealthy effects of religious instruction.

10

'Lilith! Let me help you!'

All the way up the motorway that Saturday, he practised his first speech. 'Mrs Collett!' he'd start off. And then, taking a personal initiative, 'Lilith! It might seem strange that I'm the one who's come to talk to you today. But it makes sense to me, since I've always believed we had something in common.'

– And that, of course, was William. She had put up with him for the first twenty-four years, Caspar for the last five. And putting up with William was no joke. Caspar could hardly imagine that he had changed much in the last few years. Presumably she, too, had suffered the relentless trail of fads and enthusiasms, the precipitate dives into one potential life's work after another. Caspar remembered with a shudder the months that William spent 'finding his feet as an artist'. The awful friends he'd made. The unspeakable places he'd dragged Caspar to look at 'urban sculpture *in situ*'. The frightful rubbish he'd expected Caspar cheerfully to display in his flat. It had practically come as a relief when William's attention switched without warning to the career as a composer it seemed he'd always felt was his true bent. Caspar paid for the music lessons. (One working instrument at least was *de rigueur*.) And William made fast progress through the grades, practising for hours every day. But when his efforts at the vital qualifying exam were rewarded, twice over, not with the Distinction he needed, but only with the Merit he deserved, the desire to compose suddenly appeared as provisional as the various music schools' offers, and William took up instead with cordon bleu cookery, and visions of a chain of small, discreet restaurants.

Here, Caspar put his foot down. Yes, he was quite financially secure. Rich, he was not. And what he earned, he'd never been disposed to spend on anything risky. Not the type. So William stayed home and sulked, and Caspar held out, and gradually it dawned on both of them that William was not so much a young man in search of a niche in life as one who was already comfortably in one. He still had his passions, yes. (A more disparaging man than Caspar might have referred to them as crazes.) He learned to juggle and he learned to mime. The party clown business trailed on for some months before the day William stomped home in such a foul mood that his routine announcement of 'Never again!' remained staunchly in force through all future blandishments from the agency (who later turned very nasty indeed about the state of the returned costumes). The metal 'hunting trophy' hat and coat hooks he took to making afterwards sold well (to friends). And William's foray into imported wooden joke ties from Nepal provided one lavish New Year cruise. But, on the whole, William was better off without a job. There was far less sighing and whingeing. Where the hours of his days went, Caspar had no idea. Sometimes it struck him, on return from work, that literally nothing had been done. William's capacity for sloth was so prodigious that, in anyone else, Caspar might have been tempted to make a provisional diagnosis of depression. But that was clearly not the case here. William's moods were the healthiest thing about him. They shot up and down. They swung round and around. One day he'd be feeling ineffably martyred. The next tender and generous. The next idly bored. Clearly the emotional clockwork was in tip-top repair. It was Caspar (thought Caspar) who sometimes found himself dragging his carcass through one day after the next, wondering about life's purpose and feeling almost sanguine about its end.

Had Mrs Collett found her son a strain? Or had William merely picked up his patterns of behaviour from her, so that, now he'd moved up from second billing to star, he just assumed that it was right and fitting that his needs and feelings, rather than anyone else's, should always gain the day? Perhaps these were simply bad habits he'd inherited, impinging his moods on Caspar, insisting on being the focus of attention at all times, and judging the depth of Caspar's affection by the speed and intensity of his response. If Caspar had lost a patient, he could be sure that William would lay claim to having had a particularly trying day. The week Caspar's unanswered correspondence spilled over the edge of the relief carton he'd set, in desperation, beneath his desk, William spent several evenings in a row fretting and pouting about the quality of their relationship, complaining about how long it was since they had been on holiday, and detailing at quite extraordinary length how much he'd given up to spend these thankless years in Caspar's company. It was as if, after having been outshadowed all through childhood, William was determined nothing and no one would ever outshadow him again.

And all the strain of it fell on Caspar. William had few friends. Like all his other enthusiasms, they came in waves, and so long as they were happy to dedicate themselves to William and his concerns, they were made welcome and treated generously. As soon as they transgressed, removing the focus of their attention from his needs and desires even briefly, they found themselves summarily dismissed, after which William kept Caspar awake for hours dissecting their failings and attributing to even the kindest of them the worst motives for attempting any friendship in the first place. (On the rare occasions on which Caspar dared try and steer these conversations round to how some related aspect of William's own behaviour affected him, the sessions ended instantly, in sulks or in uproar.)

So was it bad habit, or pathology? Was there some neglected, permanently-damaged toddler within William who truly feared that, if no one was paying him attention, he didn't exist? Or had he just been raised in the shadow of such relentless self-pity and absorption that he too, on first being given a home of his own and his big chance, cloistered himself in utter egotism? And what was Caspar supposed to do? Pity him? Or be revolted? More and more, recently, thought Caspar, feeling the tensions within him increase rather than slacken as he pulled off the busy motorway on to the tranquil road that led to Fellaham, it had become a bloody toss-up.

Gesturing towards the next road sign to Little Furley, he tried again.

'Lilith! I know how desperately upsetting for you all this has been . . .'

No. He wouldn't be able to come out with it. He'd choke on the words. After all, nothing about Barbara meant anything to Mrs Collett. Neither her future nor her happiness were of any concern. Caspar had heard enough over the years to know that Mrs Collett's self-interest was impregnable. If you took her line on things, as communicated by her thin and watery smiles of disbelief, and her contemptuous I-think-I-know-better-than-that looks, then Gilly had married Angus, not out of love, but simply to vex her mother with a feckless and unpresentable son-in-law. Tory and George had only moved back to Fellaham from London so they could more easily impose on her as an unpaid nanny for the twins. And William's only reason for moving in with Caspar was to set his poor father's corpse spinning in its grave. You could forgive Mrs Collett for the mean-spiritedness life had dealt her, Caspar reflected. But it was hard not to blame her for the chunks of it she passed on. And it was no comfort whatsoever to be assured she made herself at least as miserable as she made others. That crippling inability to see things from anyone else's point of view (tragically inherited by William) not only made her incapable of experiencing any of the more cheering emotions, like admiration or gratitude, but also propelled her into swathes of infuriating amnesia whenever conscience was concerned. Barbara had shown the most extraordinary self-control when Mrs Collett's few brief visits to Hector wheezing his way towards death in his side ward became transposed, as if by magic, with Barbara's month-long vigil, day and night. William had considerably more trouble buttoning his beak when the beloved tabby she so cavalierly packed off on a terminal visit to the vet one day after an accident on one of her best rugs became, when it suited her, 'poor little Bede, who died'. She had, thought Caspar, a prodigious gift for both the manipulation and the invention of facts. The phrase, 'Oh, no, dear. It wasn't at all like that,' was

practically her watchword. And so disproportionate was
her anger whenever she was questioned, that none of her
offspring ever stood up to her. Caspar could understand
it. He'd seen that even the mildest attempt to correct her
on any issue, no matter how trivial, no matter how distant,
elicited an almost allergic reaction. It was like watching
someone fall into a sort of psychic anaphylactic shock.
And after a while, he had come round to thinking, along
with the rest of them, that brushing with Mrs Collett
wasn't worth the fuss ('fuss' being defined, so far as
Caspar could make out, as any fall-out from her feeling in
the least bit gainsaid, let alone thwarted). His reasons for
not bothering hardly differed from those of her children.
They'd come, from bitter experience, to the conclusion
that few issues were worth the effort and humiliation of
having to try and win her round again. And Caspar, too,
tended to ask himself, what was the point? The answer
came promptly enough: very little, since she so dependably
combined a compulsion to stake all possibility of social
tranquillity on her being totally in the right with an
absolute incapacity to accept that she might, ever, be the
tiniest bit in the wrong.

So, year by year, he'd watched them all pretending to
be deaf, and simulating indifference to her self-serving
reinventions of their history. And maybe they were right,
and truth didn't merit the emotional storms she so tire-
lessly whipped up around her in her perpetual self-defence.
It was hard, after all, to imagine someone like Gillyflower
nailing her ninety-five theses to the door at Wittenberg, or
saying firmly, 'Here I stand.' But what about Tory? She
got in enough of a pet about issues like over-sprayed
apples and animals in cages and cuts in public transport.

How come she just fell in with tiptoeing round her mother like some maid in a French farce putting up with a tiresome old trout who could never say 'Please', or 'Thank you', let alone the real heart-softeners, like 'I am sorry', 'You were right', 'I was wrong'?

Because she knew her mother was half mad, that's why. Because, like the rest of them, she intuitively knew that Mrs Collett's infinitely intricate constructions to put and keep herself always firmly in the right would fall like a house of cards if the harsh wind of irrefutable correction blew in on just one corner. The reason why the woman responded to even the most trivial challenge, the smallest contradiction, with Chicken Licken frenzy was because something inside her truly feared, if she was wrong, the skies would fall.

'Lilith! About this wedding . . .'

Oh, it was hopeless. He felt sick with fear. The muscles across his stomach knotted as the heavy gates reared up before him: Archway to Hell. Reversing back fast into the lane (a skill he found constantly improving with practice), Caspar left the car and hung about the entrance to the Partridge for a few calming drags on his cigarette before he could even bring himself to sidle back to the gateway and peer inside. Anyone home? No small figure hacking away like a fury at some defenceless climbing plant? Caspar sighed, and looked round the garden. Without William at his side irritating him mightily from his bottomless well of mingled reminiscence and nostalgia, Caspar quite liked the look of the place. Personally, he had always preferred a tidier garden. It might be the influence of growing up opposite a solid brick wall, but there was something to be said for being able to see from one end of the lawn to the greenhouse, and from the toolshed to the stripped side wall. Some of the flowering bushes did look a little odd, he'd admit, cut back till they resembled cabbages on stalks. And it was a shame about the weigela, sheared to its stumps. But what the hell. At least you could whip round the place on a mower in no time. None of that finicky weaving in and out round precious blossom-laden stems, and having to lift great heavy spreading sprays of greenery run riot, to trim beneath. Coolly, Caspar leaned back against the gatepost, comparing the barren waste in front of him with the photographs William sometimes pulled out of his treasure box to snivel over for an hour or two. Okay, so once the laurel rose in towers, lilacs cascaded and the flowerbeds brimmed. So what? So bloody what? The only thing those heaps of greenery had done for the little Colletts, growing up in leafy wonderland, was put them in thrall to their mother for life. As long as she'd been able to stand, axe raised, over yet another intriguing little overgrown corner they used to love, she'd been able to compel their attention and demand their obedience. Like some Lord High Executioner lifting a sword over their Best Beloved, she'd had them trapped.

So why was she suddenly letting her power go, ceding it to next door for thirty shillings of silver? Didn't she *realize*? Maybe she did. Maybe she'd tired of ruling this particular roost, and had decided, as coolly and deliberately as Caspar had decided to collude with her, that it was time to have done.

Well, he was grateful to her. He'd be the last to throw a spanner in her works. He wasn't going to ring the Planning Department, or get English Heritage to invoke their emergency powers, or ask for an interview with the nearest

Sites and Monuments officer. If the price of love was a heap of old Roman remains, then so be it. Let them go, along with the scrag end of what had once been the most beautiful garden. As soon as the whole lot was razed, there'd be no more nightmares, either for Caspar or William. There might be a few weeks of weeping – salutary period of grief – then William would grow up at last. He'd understand he had no home to which he could return, sleeping or waking. No Cold Domain, no old domain. He would be Caspar's at last, body and soul.

Just at that moment, he finally noticed her. She was tucked away in one of the very few spots in the garden that still didn't offer a clear view. Her body was tensed, exerting all the force it could muster as she violently shook the trunk of the last surviving prunus, determined to fetch down the few wayward, stubborn, clinging blossoms that still resisted her.

In an instant, Caspar had ground his cigarette underfoot and sprung forward. This time it didn't even cross his mind to worry what to say. His call across the garden came out with all the fluency of perfect candour.

'Lilith! You mustn't do it by yourself! Let me help you!'

I I

'*Uninvited guests*'

'. . . naturally found it all terribly hurtful.'

'Naturally,' soothed Caspar, accepting the flowery porcelain bowl she offered him, though it was years since he'd put sugar in his coffee.

'After all,' said Mrs Collett, 'I was only thinking about Barbara. Nothing would give me greater pleasure than to see her safely married . . .'

The drifting pause, with its attendant faraway look, was held long enough for Caspar to realize that he was supposed to fill in the next bit.

'Off your hands at last.'

'It's not as if she's been an *easy* daughter.'

'I should think not,' said Caspar, getting into his stride. 'I seem to recall William mentioning a very difficult period – some fellow from a local garage?'

Mrs Collett rewarded him with her most theatrical shudder.

'Not to *mention* the trouble with that Bernard!'

Caspar nodded his sympathy as she went on to explain.

'Naturally, I was anxious. Nobody likes to see their precious daughter let down in public a third time.' She turned the doe eyes of concern on Caspar. 'After all, when she came out with the announcement, none of us had even met him.'

'That's right.'

'He could have been *anybody*.'

Leaning forward conspiratorially, she tapped him on the knee, and in a flash it was brought home to him what an astonishing difference it made not having William at his side to remind her of the cast of his sexual proclivities. They were getting on brilliantly together, cosy as toast. Why, she was practically flirting with him now.

'A woman has to be very careful. Any woman. You might not believe it, Caspar –' and here she stopped for the statutory self-deprecating little laugh '– but even I have my admirers! The trouble with Barbara, of course, is that in these matters she is still a child. She'll take anyone at their face value.'

'Even a foreigner.'

It just slipped out. He couldn't help it. Had he gone too far?

No. She was patting his knee again.

'Exactly. Even a foreigner.'

Get on with it, Caspar told himself. Go on. Before you bugger things up good and proper.

'Lilith,' he said, dropping his hand on hers, 'I've met this Miguel-Angel several times now. And, really, I think you would approve. He's very pleasant in his looks and his manners. Old-fashioned, even. And he's wonderful with Barbara. You'd hardly recognize her for the same girl.'

You wouldn't either. If he weren't paying attention, he might walk past her in the street. She would no longer trigger any unconscious associations with the old Barbara. Her shape was different, her waddle gone, her wardrobe utterly transformed, and as for that pretty, smiling face –

'She's quite radiant.'

Now he had certainly gone too far. Mrs Collett unprimped her lips just long enough to say, with transparent falsity,

'I'm delighted to hear it.'

'The thing is,' said Caspar, hastily pressing on, 'the wedding can't take place without you. We're all agreed on that.'

'Oh, really?'

Astonishing, how much sheer scorn could drip from two little words. Caspar was silent momentarily, lost in some perverse variant of admiration, and, thinking she had him nicely on the spot, Mrs Collett took the opportunity to put him right on one thing.

'I'm afraid Victoria and Gillian agree with me that, in the circumstances, there's no question of my attending a wedding at which it was made so clear I'm not welcome.'

'That was just Barbara getting excited,' said Caspar. 'She didn't really mean it then, and she certainly doesn't mean it now.'

'I don't think that either of my other two daughters believes that.'

Caspar leaned forward.

'Are you telling me neither of them is coming either?'

He could tell from the smile on Mrs Collett's face that she'd taken his pantomime astonishment totally on trust.

'Well, naturally, their loyalties are torn . . .'

He hoped the vexation in his voice sounded poorly suppressed, rather than manufactured.

'But Barbara assumed she hadn't heard from Tory because she still hadn't decided whether to get a sitter for the twins. And she thought Gilly just didn't know about Angus's shifts yet.'

The old bag! You could practically hear her purring with pleasure.

'Oh, no, Caspar. I think you'll find it's a little more than that keeping them from responding.'

'Dear me,' said Caspar. 'Oh, that is a shame. I think we'd all hoped things wouldn't reach this pass.'

Mrs Collett scratched at a thread on the sleeve of her smart woollen jacket.

'I'm sure there's no problem, Caspar. You'll all have the loveliest time at Barbara's wedding. There's certainly no need for anyone to spoil the day worrying about two or three uninvited guests.'

'You aren't uninvited,' said Caspar. 'Tory and Gilly-flower's invitations are already sitting on their mantel-pieces, and I've been asked to come today and invite you.'

The silence with which this announcement was greeted made the inadequacy of the arrangement more than clear.

With the scrupulous insistence of the heavily armed, Caspar offered her one last chance to surrender quietly.

'Please, Lilith. Come to the wedding.'

'I don't think I can, Caspar. Not in the circumstances.'

Caspar drew out of his pocket the one last tiny blue lump of mosaic he hadn't returned to Barbara. He tipped it idly from palm to palm.

'What a shame,' he repeated. 'Because I think we're all agreed that, without you three, we can hardly go ahead. Not at the price.'

He tossed the mosaic a few inches in the air.

'The price?' she said, without taking her eyes off it.

'Well, be reasonable,' said Caspar. 'One would have to have a heart as hard as *stone* –'

He flipped it. Her eyes flickered with it, up and down.

'– not to put Barbara's happiness on such a special occasion before some hazy abstract like civic duty or one's responsibilities towards archaeological research.'

Her eyes met his.

'But if the day's going to be a total wash-out anyhow . . .'

Sighing, he stuffed the mosaic back in one pocket and pulled from the other the plastic-coated notice of the planning application he'd had the foresight to remove from next door's gatepost.

She stared at the frayed lengths of official tape he'd sawn through so laboriously with his nail scissors.

'I shouldn't think this is the relevant address at all,' Caspar all but mused at her as he flattened the notification out on his knee. 'For something as important as this, it'll probably be the Ministry of Works, or some such.'

He folded it up again, more neatly.

'Never mind. These people will know.'

They gazed into one another's eyes so deeply, and for so long, that any onlooker might have thought them lovers. Then Mrs Collett murmured,

'Perhaps, on reflection . . .'

Caspar reached out to pat her hand with real warmth.

'I'm delighted. And Barbara will be *thrilled*.' He reached for his jacket. 'I'll leave you to get in touch with Tory and Gillyflower, shall I? Find out how everything's going with babysitters, and Angus's shifts, and all that?'

Nodding in dumb obedience, she started to stack the coffee cups tidily on the tray.

'I am delighted,' Caspar said again. He crushed the planning notice in his hand. 'I'll get rid of this for you,' he told her. 'After all, you don't want it blowing out of your dustbin, and people thinking that you tore it down.'

In victory, he was generous.

'Not that anybody who matters will spot that it's disappeared,' he said. 'Judging by Barbara, who hasn't even noticed it's been there.'

She glanced up from her tinkling porcelain.

'Really,' he assured her.

Their eyes met for the last time. Then Caspar clattered off, tossing lies about traffic patterns and extra Saturday clinics over his shoulder. Slowed by the weighty tray he hadn't offered to take off her hands, she let him go, only pausing by the window seat halfway along the hall to watch him stride the last few paces into the centre of the sunlit lawn, and then, astonishingly for a man his age, turn a perfect valedictory cartwheel of triumph.

12

Cartwheels. Daisies

When Lilith Collett laid her hand on the exact spot of ground where Caspar had pressed down his foot, hard, to launch himself up and over, she hardly had her son's lover in mind at all. She was thinking of cartwheels in general. It had been such a garden for cartwheels. There had been crazes of them, year after year, associated in her memory always with daisies. She could track all their lives by cartwheels. It must be forty years since she'd last bothered, then dared, to turn one. Hector couldn't be teased into having a go very much longer, not with the way his back went. And, after that, each of the children went through their own personal cycle of clumsy tumbling, followed by perfect control, then gradual ragged recession. She doubted if a single one of them could turn a cartwheel now, let alone the whole dizzy strings of them she was forever being begged to watch. 'Don't go back in, Mum! Look at me! Look at me!'

Strange how one person's pleasure is so inextricably linked to their tyranny over another. She couldn't bear to go through even a shadow of that again. Time to move on. There would be those who called her selfish, of course. 'Oh, what a shame to get rid of that beautiful garden just as your grandchildren are getting to the age to enjoy it.'

Well, bugger them. Hector would not have cared to hear her put it that way, of course. One of the few things he really disliked was that sort of language from women. But no other way of saying it was strong enough. Over the last few years, the garden had changed from a haven of escape, a place to slip away and take a few lungfuls of fresh air and be alone (if only for a few moments before she was tracked down) to being a source of unpleasantness, a symbol of strife, and an excuse for each of her endlessly demanding children to try and keep her in thrall. Why, you could barely pick up a watering can without Tory grinding up her green moral gears. 'Is that Nullweed you're using? Didn't you read that article I sent you about its high levels of poisonous residue? Why don't you just plant potatoes to clear the ground?' 'But you *can't* have got rid of that beautiful wooden water butt! George *told* you he'd fix all the leaks in it as soon as he found the time.' Walking round the garden with Tory was like going round factory plant with an inspector. Though even that was preferable to strolling round with Gillyflower. Gillyflower drove her mad. 'Oh, Mum! Do you remember when Tory and I had those wonderful little picnics under the magnolia? What happened to that doll's tea set? Is it still in the cellar? It was bright blue tin –'

And lead painted, probably, as Tory would have been the first to point out, censorious as ever, when Lilith tipped the few remaining pieces in a box, and packed them off to one of the jumble sales run by the local Scout pack. William had been a Boy Scout, for all the good it had done him. You could scarcely call living with Caspar being clean in thought, word and deed. Especially not in deed. Sometimes Lilith found herself wondering just what her son and Caspar did to one another in bed. Then she'd remember that, from what she'd read, they probably didn't do whatever it was in a bed anyhow. And as for some of the things in those leaflets Barbara had left, oh so

very tactfully, round the house after William 'came out' −
(stupid expression! so fey! so utterly *ludicrous*! and as if she
hadn't known − known for *years*) − well, they not only
disgusted her beyond any power of expression, but they'd
probably also done their bit to contribute to Hector's
early death. She'd not forget the night she woke to find
him gone from her side, and, hearing the muffled crying,
crept along the landing to the bathroom and found him
sitting so pitifully with his pajama bottoms around his
ankles, sobbing his poor heart out, with all the brightly
coloured shreds of photograph scattered across the tiles.
She'd packed him back to bed at once, and talked him
into sufficient steadiness of mind to fall asleep again. Then
she'd lain wide awake herself, till, after an hour or more of
staring at slow dawn, she'd given up, and spent the hours
till breakfast picking the tiny shreds of paper one by one
out of the dustpan and fitting them together like a jigsaw
on the kitchen table till William's patchwork face smiled
chirpily back at her from Hector's favourite school photo.
She'd never say it. No, she'd never say it. But William
going gay − and they could curl their lips at her all they
liked, but she still believed there was an element of *choice*
in people's lives − Will's going gay had signed the death
warrant for his father.

And it hadn't done that much for him. When did you
ever see him smiling now? He turned up on his lordly
visits, trailing that creepy perverted slug Caspar behind
him, and if you so much as lifted the secateurs to snip off
some rogue shoot, he was down your throat. 'There'll be
none left if you go on like that!' What was it about her
children? How had they all turned out so constipated
about change? There wasn't a single one of them who

would voluntarily alter anything about this place. Look at
the fuss the day she painted the hall a slightly different
shade of blue! The squawking when she threw out those
horrid old planters! They seemed to think they had the
right to keep things exactly how they always were. When
she asked Barbara – (age thirty-two; not *twenty*-two: *thirty*-
two) – to move the last of her stuff to the clinic where,
after all, she had a room and had been working for *years*,
her face crumpled, and somehow she managed to look as
if she had been *slapped*. But it was hardly Lilith's fault if,
after ten years in charge of the hospital's principal unit,
Barbara couldn't insist on having slightly better accommodation with a bit more storage space. Why, after all,
should Lilith have to run her house for the convenience of
Fellaham District Health Authority? If she wanted a
couple of uncluttered bedrooms, that surely was her pre-
rogative. It was her house, after all. Why should she have
to put up with William's dismembered sports cars rusting
away in the garage, and upstairs cupboards stuffed to
bursting with Barbara's stupid teddies and Gilly's favourite jigsaws? Even Victoria seemed to presume she had the
right to take up all of the only truly weatherproof outdoor
shed with her boxes of art equipment and clay bins and
easels. 'Just till George gets round to finishing the extension.' Just till pigs fly! Did they think she should run her
life around them for ever? They were in for a shock, then.
A necessary shock. Lilith could still recall the jolt it had
given her years ago when Mrs Maxwell lifted her head
from the silver she'd been so discreetly continuing to
polish, and said to young Mrs Philimore from next door,
in tears from her most recent beating, 'You ought to leave
that man. I'm sure your mother and father didn't go to

the trouble of having you and raising you, just so you could become Roderick Philimore's punch bag.' The observation had meant little to silly Harriet. Within a week, she was rushing into Lilith's kitchen again, freshly bruised, copiously weeping. But it had forcibly struck home in Lilith's mind. From that day on, the tiny and subversive thought took root. Was I put on this planet to make Hector Collett happy? No, I was not. And the tiny resentful feeling had grown like a cancer, encompassing the children, making the difficult impossible, and spoiling all of married life. What *mistakes* women made, attempting to atone for each and every small ungenerous impulse with ludicrous offers of further self-sacrifice. The trouble was that no one could ever truly imagine how very long, how very fine, the wheel of life was going to grind. In that respect, it was like childbirth. If you could reach out and press a button to stop it all happening once it got rough, few enough babies would be born. And fewer still would grow to adulthood if, similarly, a woman could call a clean halt when suddenly she realized this was it. This was the deal. Her whole life chewed up thoroughly – and then old age.

Some women, it suited. (Just enough, perhaps.) Oh, lucky, lucky women! For others, like her, it was a grim constricting fate that pinched their natures and soured their tempers. And nothing could alter it. No change of circumstance. No force of will. Over the years, she must have told herself a hundred thousand times: Lilith, *relax*. Enjoy your children and treasure the garden. Let worries roll over you, and be at peace.

And what good had it done her? None. It wasn't in her. It was so little in her that she couldn't last a single, solitary morning. Within an hour, some duty would be nagging at her mind, and she'd be filled with the unholy rage of resentment. Why *should* she have to answer that ringing phone? (Because one of them might be in hospital, crying for her, that's why.) Or let out that scrabbling cat? (Because opening a door is less trouble than scrubbing a rug later.) Or do *this*? Or do *that*? Or the never-ending *other*?

The savagely plucked heads of the daisies flew. Lilith looked down to find herself staring at filthy, grass-streaked fingers. Oh, God! How many times a day did these hands go under the tap? More than enough to outshine Lady Macbeth. Stuck on the modern treadmill of birthdays and Christmas and New Year and Easter, that infamous mother and housewife would never have found the time to wish Duncan anything more sinister than simply gone from her house. 'And then it's Banquo's birthday next week, dear. And Donalbain's the week after. And surely some of Macduff's pretty ones were born in August. Do I have to buy them all presents? Or shall I just give them cards?'

Or *murder* them. Digging her fingers deep, till soil impacted painfully under her nails, Lilith tore out a clump of dandelion and hurled it in the nearest bush. Even when people were dead, you weren't allowed to drop them from the list of tyrannies. Hector had been buried ten years. Ten years! And still, inexorably, in the first week of March, Barbara showed up on the doorstep with that ghastly professional look of sympathy stuck all over her face, and some expensive delicacy under her arm, wanting to be part of it. But part of *what*? Hector was *gone*. Barbara could gripe down the phone to William all she liked about the lack of warmth in her mother's reception, the absence of basic human gratitude. (Oh, yes! She'd realized years ago why their two lines were yoked for hours after these occasions.) But it was Barbara who was being selfish. Barbara! Like all the rest of the bloodsuckers draining Lilith dry, Barbara was just determinedly pressing on with some old pattern of life in which the second day of March was Hector's birthday. She was refusing to get on with the new, when he was dead and buried – *gone*. Lilith had learned to leave her to it. If Barbara wanted to play the same little game every spring, then she was welcome. But she wouldn't fool anyone, let alone the real widow. For Lilith had learned one cold, hard fact over the last ten years, and it was this. If, after using up the best of her, Hector could not even manage to stay alive to see her through some of the worst, she couldn't mourn him. No. Not any more.

Anyhow, she hadn't time, not with the rest of them at her all day with their demands. 'You haven't been over for ages.' 'Why don't you come to the pantomime with me and the children?' 'I can't *believe* that you and Fran have never met. She's been my closest friend for *years*.' And very nice too, if she could summon up the energy to take an interest in their new flats and carpets, their children and their friends. But she was burned out. She was just a husk. The Herculean task of suppressing all her unmotherly responses had drained her till there was nothing left. She'd spent a lifetime taking care not to say too many curt things: 'Get off!' 'Stop clinging!' 'Make up your *own* mind.' 'Can't you even do a cartwheel without me having to stand and admire you?' 'For God's sake, leave me *alone*!' 'Go *away*!' And maybe she'd been wrong, and it was the sheer effort of muzzling herself for thirty years that had bled away her strength, and left her without sufficient energy even to make a decent show of cooing over her grandchildren's bright poster paint daubs, or admiring the way they crashed round the stage at the nursery school, wearing their cardboard bunny ears and getting the words of their song wrong.

It was a tragedy, but there you are. Few people's lives make merry stories, start to end. And at least she was getting out soon. None of the children yet knew about the deposit on the compact little bungalow at the far end of Frosthole Close, and they'd be horrified when they saw it. She could hear them already. 'But where will you put the piano?' 'You can't sell Granny's wonderful old dresser!' 'And what am I supposed to do with all that stuff of mine that's in your garage?' No wonder she'd left telling them until the last minute. They'd make the usual fuss. But she was determined to go through with this. That's why she'd been so appalled to hear about Barbara's wedding. Dismantling a family home after forty years was a huge undertaking, and she couldn't afford another of Barbara's hysterical disappointments and series of scenes when the man in her life suddenly realized where he was heading, and prudently turned tail. And even if this one was, quite remarkably, to stay the course, the sheer inconvenience of having the wedding party at Cold Domain made it out of the question. They would be in and out all the time, dumping gifts, measuring serving tables, discussing flowers. Sooner or later they'd be bound to realize what was going on. The postman would hand them an envelope stamped by Land Registry. Or they'd bump into some surveyor in the garden. Or one of the neighbours would blab. This was an undertaking to last weeks. First, get the planning permission safely in hand. Then sign the papers selling the land to the man taking over the Partridge. Then sell the house. She couldn't manage it with Barbara and Gilly-flower weeping and wailing about old childhood treasures missing from the cellar, and Tory railing at her for doing it at all, or for doing it all wrong, and William egging Caspar on to law to try and stop her, or, worse, wasting months and months in some futile attempt to raise the wherewithal to buy house and garden off her. It was a sensible decision to tell them only afterwards, when it was done and there was no going back. And if they wanted to get in a huff and not speak to her any longer, so much the better. She would be halfway to her goal: a bit of peace. Without the four of them turning up on her doorstep time and again trailing their tears and memories and gardening strictures, she'd have the time to put the last remaining scrap of her energy into the last remaining scrap of herself.

If she wasn't double-crossed by that Caspar. What was the slippery bastard up to now? He must be planning to betray her or William. One or the other of them. It must be her. What would he have to gain in stabbing William in the back? She didn't flatter herself that he enjoyed his visits to Cold Domain, but it was hard to credit that they were so utterly miserable that they merited helping her do away with the garden. He was a wily fellow, who let not his left hand know what his right hand was doing. When it first dawned on her that he was offering Barbara a wedding at the Partridge, she had assumed that he knew everything. After he'd gone, and she'd had time to think, she had decided he was meddling simply from spite, and only bad luck had made him settle on the Partridge. Now that he'd spent the afternoon making it clear that he not only knew about her plans, but knew how to put a stop to them with one single phone call, she didn't know what to think – except, of course, that now both the guilt and the responsibility had been miraculously halved.

Caspar and Lilith. Strange thought. Unholy alliance. But it might serve, if Caspar's mysterious intentions held firm. She mustn't worry. He might even help. He clearly wasn't pressing Barbara to come round and make her usual noisy, breast-beating peace. He'd made it plain a gracious agreement to attend the festivities would be sufficient. And he'd successfully kept William away for several weeks. Only three more to go to that vital Land Use committee meeting two days before Barbara's wedding – a busy week, in which Barbara would voluntarily clang the iron doors of household responsibility closed on herself just as her mother finally pushed them open.

Lilith stretched back luxuriously on the daisy-studded lawn, and gazed up at the sky. Nobody realized it, but people her age had dreams. And hers was on its way. A tiny house (not really safe for grandchildren, too cramped for guests) where she could finally cast off the nail-hard shell behind which what little of herself was left had been so arduously protected. She could be kind now. She could be soft, and generous, and loving. She could have been Mrs Benevolent all her life, if she hadn't been trapped into being Mrs Collett. But her real life was starting in three weeks.

Three weeks . . .

As Lilith gazed up, filled with the tremulous longing of any prisoner in his last days, a huge steely cloud rolled over the heights of the sycamore, and hid the sun.

13

Boy

The selfsame cloud burst over Caspar as he swung his car off the roundabout and down the slip-road on to the motorway. He made it his excuse for stopping for the hitchhiker, though he'd been picking up road strays for years.

And this one was a cracker. Caspar could feel the pressure against his flies even before their eyes met. There was none of that nerve-racking will-he-or-won't-he, either. The boy reeked of sex and submission. The boy was his before the half-empty sodden rucksack had been tossed on the back seat, before the car had slid off the hard shoulder, before the seat belt was snapped into place.

Caspar drove fast, and barely spoke except to mutter through the rain-swilled arc in front of him about the tiresome prudence of all the other drivers. He didn't want to get to know the boy. He didn't want to learn which sixth form college he was attending, what subjects he was studying for his exams, and where he planned to go afterwards. He was coming to London with Caspar, and that was enough. Knowing too much would spoil it.

And it was obvious the boy understood. He must have come across Caspar's sort often enough, after all, trolling up and down motorways with almost nothing in his bag, and a stance you could spot through a cloudburst. None the less, as they neared the first series of flyovers Caspar did take the precaution of checking, asking where in the city he was headed, and responding to the boy's incon-sequential murmurs and vague shrug with the casual, 'Want to come back with me for a while?'

But where? Caspar no longer took anyone to the flat. For all the fine words spoken when the arrangement with William was set up, the price paid in tantrums on the few occasions he'd tried it had always proved far too high. Cheaper in every sense to go to that hotel on Seddon Street, behind the hospital.

And that is where he drove. Cheap, clean and quiet (by which Caspar meant proper walls, no thin partitions or connecting doors) and no problem with the parking. The boy barely glanced round on their way up the stairs, though it looked like indifference rather than nervousness. A pity the few toys that Caspar enjoyed from time to time were back in the flat with William. But never mind. Perhaps there would prove to be something useful in the rucksack . . .

The afternoon astonished even Caspar. It was a revela-tion, from the tiny skilled pause of provocation before the boy responded to Caspar's first 'On your knees, please,' to the accomplished way he blanked out his pale eyes and called his heavily handled body to order through Caspar's relentless and implacable demands. The sheer pliant beauty of such a young, growing body was always discon-certing. What came as more of a surprise was how much sharp pleasure could be exchanged with one thick leather belt, a clever little trinket from a key ring, and a boy who knew how to open his mouth only to use it properly, or say 'Sir'.

After, Caspar felt generous. Even while feeling in his pocket for his wallet, he was nodding at the typed sheet

pinned on the door. 'You're welcome to use the room till
noon tomorrow.'

Embarrassed, the boy shook his head.

'Better get on.'

He'd nearly said, 'Better get back,' and Caspar knew it.
His mother would probably be exclaiming over his absence
by ten o'clock, and fussing with tinfoil so that his supper
didn't dry to a crust in the oven, while she tried not to
think the unthinkable. Like Mrs Collett all those years
ago, the mother of this boy must lie awake, rigid with
anxiety, while her son cruised up and down the motorways, chatting to strangers, waiting with equal hope and
fear for the tell-tale hand to fall on his thigh. Had William
given such good service in his own time (and in his own
way)? Probably. Perfect young flesh was perfect young
flesh, after all. Now surely even he would feel a tremor of
awe, laying hands on this body.

Caspar's rush of generosity deepened to gratitude.

'Come on,' he said. 'Let me give you a lift back to the
motorway.'

The boy didn't even try and pretend. Nodding his
thanks, he lifted his jacket off the back of the chair, and
unlatched the door. Caspar surreptitiously fingered the
remaining notes in his wallet as he followed the glorious
high-riding buttocks down the stairs, and round the side
of the hotel, to the car. The traffic was as dire as he had
known it would be, but he didn't mind. It gave him more
time to work out his story for William. The boy, merci-
fully, passed the time in silence, doing nothing more
intrusive than experimentally raising and lowering his
seat back. Caspar drove a good ten miles out of the city,
to drop him at the likeliest place for a lift home. Then, in

a fit of good cheer, he pressed another few banknotes into his hand.

'Buy yourself something nice.'

The boy grinned, almost as if, like Caspar, he was already envisaging tomorrow's lorry driver, who would take so much pleasure in bruises already darkening, weals already raised on that cool, porcelain bum. He slammed the door so hard the crumpled planning notice that had slid to the floor through all his fiddling with the seat was cleanly cut in half.

Caspar pressed the button that lowered the window, and stretched out his hand. Clumsily, the boy leaned back inside to shake it. Then, in mingled relief and embarrassment, he turned away, and Caspar drove off at speed.

At the first traffic lights, he noticed people turning to stare at him, and it was a moment before he understood why. His passenger window was still wide open, and he was singing at the top of his voice.

'*Love,*' he was carolling cheerfully, '*is a many-splendoured thing . . .*'

Caspar wound up the window, but kept right on singing.

III

I

A many-splendoured thing

Barbara's dressmaker was getting quite cross with her.

'I can't believe I've got to take it in *again*.'

Barbara spun a pirouette of sheer happiness, and ended up in Miguel-Angel's arms.

'I certainly can't do it if you won't stand still!'

He handed her back to the dressmaker, who frowned and tutted as she put in the pins.

'A week on Friday. That's the soonest I can get it done.'

'But the wedding's the day after!'

'I know.' Looking at Barbara's radiant face, she relented. 'All right. Thursday. But don't come round to fetch it until the evening.'

'And you won't forget to sew the little blue bead thing into the hem.'

'I won't forget.'

Miguel-Angel turned to the wall as the dressmaker lifted the wedding gown carefully over Barbara's head. When he'd finished inspecting the photographs of other brides, other triumphs in satin and lace and velvet and chiffon, and she'd had time to step back in her skirt and button her blouse, he turned back to her, whistling softly.

'What's that?'

Ever courteous, he broke off at once.

'What?'

'The tune you're whistling.'

He only shrugged. He hadn't realized he was whistling. But the dressmaker, settling the gown on its expensive-looking padded hanger, rebuked Barbara gently.

'Silly girl. You, of all people, ought to recognize that song.'

Barbara sailed as close to peremptory as was possible for someone of her nature. To her lover, she said sternly, 'Whistle it again,' and to the dressmaker who'd become a friend, 'Go on, then. Sing the words.'

Obligingly, Miguel-Angel began again, at the beginning. The dressmaker had a fine voice.

'*Love*,' she sang, '*is a many-splendoured thing . . .*'

All of them burst out laughing. Then Barbara said:

'Oh, gosh! Will my luck hold?'

2

Right on all counts

Tory and Gillyflower trailed round the dress departments of the Fellaham shops. Tory had already decided to wear her green again, and borrow a nice hat. And Gilly had never in her whole life managed to buy a new frock with anyone watching. She couldn't bear to think of them standing waiting while she tried things on. She couldn't concentrate on what it might look like if she was wearing the right shoes, or a different shade of tights. She always ended up just running her fingers along the overstuffed racks, admiring the materials. 'That's pretty, isn't it?' 'I really like that.'

After less than an hour, they found themselves lingering longer around the china than the clothes. (Tory was after a milk jug.) Then Gilly cracked.

'If we nipped through the Food Hall, I reckon I could skip my Friday trip to Tesco's.'

Tory, who knew all along that Gilly would end up wearing her brown floral, still felt obliged to put the case for Barbara's Wedding Shop.

'Once we're loaded with groceries, we'll have to go straight back to the car.'

Gilly sighed.

'I don't mind if you don't. But what about your wedding present?'

Tory already had her foot on the stairs.

'It doesn't matter. I rather thought I might give them

that cut-glass wind chime George's aunt sent from Dublin. It's never been out of the box.'

Gilly cheered up.

'Do you think I might get away with that downie Angus won in the last Horridge raffle?'

'Why not? They're always useful.'

In celebration of the money saved, Gillyflower dumped two packets of frozen American sundaes into her trolley. (No need to diet if she wore the brown.)

'Funny thing,' she said, turning to Tory. 'Someone at Horridge's told Angus he thought that Mother's house was up for sale.'

Tory lifted a carton of eight banana yoghurts near their sell-by date off the shelf of reduced items. None of the family was crazy about banana-flavoured anything, but the difference in price was considerable.

'People do get things so mixed-up,' she said. 'Apparently it's the Partridge that's up for sale. It's been in difficulties for a while, and now it's going to some foreign firm.'

'Serves them right,' Gilly said scornfully. 'Ridiculous prices!'

Tory glanced back over her shoulder.

'A pity yoghurt doesn't freeze . . .'

'It is odd, though,' said Gillyflower. 'You keep hearing all these strange things. I don't mention them to Mother in case they upset her. But last night Angus came home saying one of the clerks had actually seen an application for planning permission for part of the garden.'

'I heard that one,' said Tory. 'Except, the way I heard it, it was for chalets next door.'

Still mightily relieved at all the money she wasn't

having to spend on Barbara's wedding, Gilly chose a shoulder of lamb above the usual bacon joint.

'Can we go back to the vegetables, just for a moment?'

Tory executed a smart three-point trolley turn.

'I reckon half people's brains drain into their socks when they pick up a local paper,' she told her sister. 'Presumably the Partridge needs permission to change hands. It is a hotel, after all. I'm sure the council has to check it's not being bought by the mafia, or a known brothel-keeper, or a professional gambling mob. One little change of ownership notice in the *Fellaham Courier*, and all this gossip starts. People are halfwits.'

She was so used to being in the right on all counts, it never struck her that she might be wrong.

3
'Right or left for comfort?'

'I'm sorry?'

William forced himself to look at the bright face beaming up at him.

'I was asking which side you dress, sir.'

Oh, God. Of course.

'Left . . . Yes. Left.'

'Very good, sir.'

The youth bent his head to tape measure and task, and William tried to quell the rush of anger and embarrassment inside him. He didn't need a new suit anyway. And, if he did, why did he have to come to this stiff-arsed establishment of Caspar's? Something nice and expensive off the peg had always done him before. Was Caspar trying to send some kind of message? Your body isn't what it used to be. It's time your suits were fitted properly.

It even rhymed! William's snort of contempt for his own desperate attempts at self-distraction unnerved the tailor's assistant.

'Sir?'

'Nothing.'

And it was nothing. After all, it wasn't Caspar's fault that this young man crouched at his feet had cousin Dougie's hair, that flaming Scottish mop that fascinated him even as a baby. 'You used to reach out between the bars of your cot, and try to grab handfuls of it.' 'Once you hacked a whole chunk off while he was asleep.' There were so many stories. The only one that William remembered, nobody ever told. Nobody guessed that, taken to watch Dougie swirl his bright scarlet cloak in the nativity play, William had fallen in love – a giant crush that lasted till that day he'd spent years forgetting.

'Just one little double-check, sir. For my peace of mind.'

Thank God the man was off his knees at last. Obediently, William raised his arm, and suddenly the stomach-churning curls were bobbing around him again.

That's how it began. A rough and tumble game, with Dougie hurling himself out of the cover of the laurels over and over again to try and roll on William's little garden and squash his pansies and snapdragons and hollyhocks, while William desperately pushed him off. It got to be a ritual, till the year Dougie's greed finally combined with William's skill at raising strawberries to make a lasting peace. Lasting, that is, until the summer Dougie, master of new games, began the rough and tumble all over again, but differently this time, and in the laurels, not out on William's garden.

What was it about Dougie? Even after all these years, William could not work out how a few swirls from a cheap muslin cloak could have put him so in thrall to his cousin. Surely it was the worst luck that one or two barked orders from a junior school Herod could raise their echoes of excitement so strongly down the years that even when William sensed his mother approaching, the mere pressure of Dougie's hand on his head had kept him meekly at his task.

Had she actually seen them? She'd burst through the

laurels with such force that she'd sent sequestered rain-drops flying. In all probability, she'd *smelt* them out. They must have *reeked* of sex. She wasn't daft.

And they were lucky, of course. For Dougie had fin-ished. He had even zipped up again. And no one could punish two young boys for looking flushed. For all she could tell, they had simply been scrapping as usual.

She knew, though. She knew. That was the only explana-tion for the look in her eyes and the terror that gripped him. He'd stumbled back into the most precious fuchsia of his new collection, the 'Abbé Farges', breaking its stems, and crushing the perfect purple bells all down one side.

'What a mess this corner's getting! I thought you promised me you'd be fully responsible for this part of the garden.'

Dougie slid away, and William couldn't blame him. But William had to stay, horror and self-disgust rising to tears as she deliberately ripped out from the laurels all the loose glorious trails of his particular pride and joy, the luscious flame flower he'd so laboriously grown from seed: *Tropaeolum speciosum*.

'There. That looks tidier.'

Never again had William had sex in the garden. Or fancied anyone with flaming hair.

The youth twirled his measuring tape back into its case.

'I don't think there'll be anything more, sir.'

William gazed evenly ahead.

Too right, boyo, he was thinking. No, there certainly won't. Not for you.

4
White suit

Miguel-Angel handed the letter back to Barbara with a look of distaste. Barbara read it again.

'*Indulge me*,' Caspar had written. And, underneath, were the directions on how to reach his tailor, and reassurances that, even at this late date, the suit could be ready on time.

'I have a suit,' Miguel-Angel said stubbornly.

'But this is for a *white* suit. He wants you in white.'

The look of distaste deepened to a scowl.

'I have a white suit.'

Barbara did try to mask her disbelief, but Miguel-Angel saw.

'At home,' he insisted. 'In a closet.'

'Could your parents bring it with them?'

Miguel-Angel shrugged.

'He's done us so many favours,' said Barbara. But she wasn't sure of her ground. Right from the start, Miguel-Angel had treated Caspar's interventions with the sort of detachment more commonly shown to a financial broker than to a benefactor. Even the reference he had made to Caspar paying the bill – 'something borrowed' – put further distance between them. But this 'indulgence' of the suit had clearly touched a nerve.

And not just in him. Barbara fought panic as, for the second time that day, it was brought home to her that she was marrying into the unknown. Broadbent had been the first to unnerve her. Only that afternoon he'd sat behind the very same desk over which Caspar had steepled his fingers at her, and he'd delivered quite a lecture about diminishing fertility and erratic ovulatory signals before telling her to slip off her skirt and hop up on the couch for him.

'Hop up'. Stupid expression. But Barbara lay radiant, knowing that, practically for the first time ever, she'd climbed up without the help of the little stool. Not only that, but she'd actually fitted on their disposable strip of paper sheet without spilling over on both sides. Barbara felt so elated the nurse had to ask her a couple of times to shift up a little, so her head was on the pillow.

And Broadbent, luckily, spent those few seconds rereading Caspar's little note. It was a different man who came to check her over. 'Matter of confidence', Caspar had suggested, and if there was one thing on which Broadbent had prided himself since the start of his career, it was in the banishing of unnecessary worries. The comforting phrases poured out. 'Can't see anything wrong here.' 'Tickety-boo.' 'No signs of trouble.' 'In fine shape.' He got so in the swing that, when he had finished, he practically had to stop himself patting her bottom.

'I honestly can't see why you should face more of a problem than any other woman your age,' he finally assured her, pressing one of the clinic's little pink basal temperature thermometers into her hand as a free gift. 'Give it a go for a few months. A little extra care with the timing, and there's no reason someone as fit as you shouldn't be successful without any further help from us.'

But then, for all Caspar's strictures, the professional in him couldn't help surfacing.

'Unless, of course, there proves to be some problem on the other side . . .'

'The other side?'

It was a moment or two before she grasped the fact that he was talking about Miguel-Angel. The shadowy figure of speech had been drawn into play because Broadbent didn't even know her fiancé's name, let alone whether he'd sailed through his adult life fecundly siring one baby after another. And, to be fair, neither did Barbara. On the occasions when the subject of his past had come up between them, he'd shown a gift for promptly steering the conversation towards his earliest years. She knew a lot about the hot clattering kitchens of his childhood, the dusty sun-blinded alleys and raucous games that took in whole strings of children and a maze of streets. She knew a little about his elementary school, far less about the next one, and almost nothing about his life after that. He'd shown her no photographs, even after all these weeks of her hints and suggestions. And even the letters tossed on his window ledge disappeared in a day or so. He was a man of secrets who never left her in his room alone. Once, only once, when he'd been called downstairs in some emergency, had she slid out the topmost drawer of his dresser. But then her heart thumped so hard it tore at her chest, and she quickly pushed it shut again. She had to trust him. She had to let small mysteries slide by. The day she'd slowed her car to a crawl, fearing a dream, when she caught sight of him in a phone box in the next village, shovelling in coins as though the mere earning of them was of no account. The night he'd draped his dressing-gown round her chilled shoulders and she could have sworn she'd heard a soft ticking and felt the smooth bulge of a fob watch through the thin fabric before, distracting her with some nonsense, he'd slid his hand in the pocket and removed it. There was the time she saw pages of closely written figures under the bed, and the time she heard the machine-gun rattle of his home-grown Spanish up the stairs when he was called to the phone. 'No trouble at home, I hope?' 'No, no. I assure you. No trouble.'

Why hadn't any of this worried her? It didn't hang together. It didn't fit. And she would never have advised one of her friends or patients to leap into an unknowable future alongside a husband with an unknown past. Like the blind act of faith she couldn't help sensing that Father O'Hare secretly (and mistakenly) hoped she might take at the end of her course of instruction, marrying Miguel-Angel would be a step in the dark. And yet she didn't mind. *Why?*

Because he had no twisty thoughts. Unlike that worm Andrew Taylor, and even Bossy Bernard, either he spoke the truth, or he was silent. Everything he said could be believed. She tried to tell herself that, for the third time in her life, she could be nine-tenths of the way to being a prize fool. He might have a wife and six children waiting in Santiago de Compostela. He might be importing crates of illegal weapons, or have his hand artfully in the till. And she couldn't believe it. His utter honesty shone through his kind hands and his gentle fingertips, his searching kisses, even the self-mockery of his frustrated groans. They could call her a madwoman if they wanted. Her faith in him was unassailable. And if they asked her how she could even think of offering the rest of her life to someone about whom she knew so little, the answer came promptly: because that's exactly what he's offering me.

Now he was turning back from his short sulk at the window.

'What are you whispering?'

He'd caught her murmuring the words of a riddle from some beloved book of fairy tales packed off for jumble many years before.

She blushed and wouldn't answer. He caught her hand and squeezed.

'Tell me.'

His grip was a lot harder than she expected.

'"What is the true price of love?"' she gasped.

Immediately, he released her hand.

'Easy,' he answered evenly. 'Always, the true price of love is love.'

Yes. Caspar was right, as usual. He was a prince. And he should be married in white.

Tears stood in her eyes when she asked him:

'Get them to bring the suit. Please. Wear it for me.'

5

On Barbara's wedding morning . . .

On Barbara's wedding morning, Mrs Collett woke to the sound of martins squabbling under the eaves. Her first thought was — a present! I haven't got them a present! She lay back on her pillows, reviewing the contents of her cupboards and shelves. There was a set of pretty tea cups in the crawl space beneath the stairs. But they weren't properly boxed. They wouldn't do. She had the string of pearls Hector had bought her for their last anniversary. But, knowing Barbara, she'd remember them. And anyhow, pearls seemed too personal a present. Could she perhaps give them a plant? Find a nice terracotta tub, and scrub it clean, and dress up whatever looked nice enough with ribbons?

And then it struck her. Perfect! The percolator! It had been sitting on a shelf in the cellar for years, still in its box. The ideal gift for a wedding, and if she didn't find a home for it soon, the rubber round its fixings would perish from sheer age. Was the plug on it round pin or square pin? She'd have to check, and switch it with another if it were necessary.

Inspirited, she slid her feet inside her slippers and padded down the stairs. The moment she started to struggle with the latch on the cellar door, the cats began yowling, desperate to go down. Lilith was more circumspect, taking her time on the uneven steps, and cursing the dimness of the lightbulb she'd chosen to 'use up' in this dark place.

There it was, though. Exactly where she remembered. The back of the box was a little discoloured where it had touched the wall, but she could probably disguise that. It felt good and heavy when she pulled it out. A perfectly adequate present. She hadn't seen anyone using this sort of percolator for a while. Mostly, now, they used filters, or those fragile glass jugs with steel stoppers you pushed down. Or even those ridiculously fancy cappucino machines she'd seen in the basement of Forrester's last Christmas.

But it would do very nicely. She'd take her time with the wrapping and the gift tag, and no one, least of all Barbara, would ever notice that it wasn't brand new.

And anyway, it was a very useful present. That's why she'd kept it so long. She'd always known that one day it would come in useful.

6

Dog's dinner

Gilly stood, stark in her underwear, in front of the bedroom mirror. From a hanger in her left hand hung the
brown floral pinafore frock she'd had for years, and, from
a hanger in her right, the slinky and expensive sheath
dress she'd borrowed from Angus's sister.

'I'd play safe and stick with the brown, dear.'

She heard the echo of the words so clear, her mother
might have been in the room. Memories came flooding.
The time she'd laboriously piled up her hair, and walked
in the kitchen to a gale of laughter. 'Oh, aren't we Miss
Macaroni? Aren't we the Big I Am?' The photo that, in a
fit of confidence, she'd sent to be enlarged for her parents'
anniversary. Some student friend had caught her laughing
in the sunshine – head tossed back, not herself at all –
someone expansive and glowing; a daughter of whom two
parents might be proud. 'Oh, dear! It makes you look all
teeth and hair!' (And then, after saying *that*, to hang it on
the wall on the upstairs landing, so that every time she
walked past –)

But memory, speeding down tracks well greased by the
master of maintenance, mortification, had finally reached
its goal. Dog's dinner. Out it came – *whoomph!* – its sockful
of wet sand catching her so hard she had to sink on to the
bedspread. Dog's dinner. Nothing to do but sit till the
horrid memory had run its course. She had been seventeen. Seventeen! Not even out of school, and yet the

passion she'd felt for Richard Clayton! Hot dreams and wobbly knees, and a fierce knocking against her ribs each time the telephone rang. The *hours* she'd spent fussing with hair, and make-up, and clothing. She could see herself now, at the table beside Tory, with her elbows stuck firmly in squeezed halves of lemon. Oh, what a mad idea! How could the elbows of a seventeen-year-old be anything short of perfection?

Richard had thought so, anyway; she was sure of that. The only time her confidence even faltered was when he pushed her between the stone pillars shadowing the monstrous front door of the house he referred to as home (for all there was a sign beside the gates, detailing opening times and prices of admission). He'd led her down hallways as long as corridors at school, introducing her proudly to everyone who crossed their path (each one of whom she would have taken for family, but for the odd chance exchange about where tea was being served, or where the fires were laid) till suddenly they were there, in the vast drawing-room. Ceilings so high you could have shouted up at them, and waited for the echo. Drapery so rich and heavy it surely had to hang for years, or go to London for cleaning. Furniture that needed the company it kept. (Each piece, marooned in any other house, would spark off tiresomely a thousand times: 'Oh, look at that! Isn't it *wonderful*! Where on earth does it come from? And how did you ever get it through the door?')

Then, striding over the rug to her, arms outstretched, was Richard's mother. Out of the swish of perfume came a quick hug and a throaty laugh. 'So this is your heavenly Gillyflower!' She had a memory of toast (a bit stale), tea (far too weak) and sitting neatly on a beaded footstool, affecting interest in a stencilled fireplace fan while family talk flashed around her. 'No, Richard, darling! Don't laugh! Poor Nana can't wriggle out of it now. It isn't any silly old party. It's practically a *command*. She has to go even if she's dropping. So, when she pops out, you just be sure to tell her how splendid she looks, or I shall send your precious Gillyflower packing, and order you off to bed!'

Was it two minutes, or twenty? She could remember talking about her school (though the quite startled look on Mrs Clayton's face when Gilly began to detail the subjects she was studying alerted her to the fact that this was not a household in which schoolwork or examinations counted for much). She had a memory of some chat about hyacinths (adored? disliked? despised? – she couldn't recall) and then, with a surprising rattle of the doorknob and a flurry of draughts round her ankles, the moment came that was now seared in memory with acid shame.

Richard's great-grandmother appeared in the doorway in a shimmer of blue. The gown was of floor length. Jewels caught the light. And there were even spangles in her hair. Could they be *diamonds*? Real *diamonds*?

'Come in. Come in.' Richard's mother was humorously ruthless. 'How can we admire you properly at such a distance?'

Would Gilly see forever the frail old lady slowly making her way towards them over the acres of carpet? For all that Richard's great-grandmother could not have differed from her more in age and looks, it came to Gillyflower suddenly that this was the very way in which she wanted to walk up the aisle towards her solemnly waiting Richard – yes, with exactly this bewitching blend of natural dignity and shy lack of assurance. Nothing else would do.

Mrs Clayton was first to speak. 'Now haven't you

managed perfectly, Nana! You look a positive dream!'
Richard was next. 'Nan, you'll be wading through broken
hearts all night!' But it was Gilly's generous and affection-
ate outburst towards this fragile stranger who had shown
her the way that rang most clearly round the room.

'You look a proper dog's dinner! You really do!'

Oh, the silence! The shock in the air. The sheer, unholy
glee in the hard, oil-painted eyes of all the Claytons
hanging on the walls. Even before the echo round the
cornices had died away, she'd guessed the truth. Everyone
stared at her, even her precious Richard. And they were
right! How could she have heard such words, such *ugly*
words, so often, and never realized what they meant?
How could she simply have assumed, not just through
buoyant and uncaring childhood, but on into tentative
and questioning adolescence, that each time she swirled
before her mother in some proud new party combination,
it was a *compliment* she was hearing, it was *praise*?

The moment passed – or she supposed it passed – while
blood pounded in her ears and behind her eyes. Gasping
inelegantly for air, she tried to stay on her feet – not howl,
not wail, not scream her desperation. She barely heard
the cool, cool dismissal. 'Now, Richard, darling, you see
Gilly safely home, while I go with Nana.'

And that was it. End of romance. End of story. Twice
she had rung to explain, and Mrs Clayton had been
graciousness itself, said she quite understood, it was nothing, Gilly was to put it out of her mind. But Richard still
failed to ring. And in a week or so she'd heard from Tory
that he'd been seen with someone else. In fewer than six
months, still smarting, still bereft of sense, she'd married
Angus just because he asked her.

But Angus proved no exorcist. She'd had to do that job alone over the years, hardening herself against *Dog's Dinner Pet Food*, and little Richard next door, and Mr Clayton, the milkman. The blows came less and less often. And gradually she even managed to believe the lie which had once utterly failed to console her: 'For heaven's sake! It probably would have happened anyway.'

Leaving her with the one, last, immutable, indissoluble pain. What sort of mother is it who so unfailingly greets your shiniest version of yourself with scorn that you take what you hear for simple approbation? What sort of childhood could it be that leaves you so unversed in praise, you don't even know the right words to pass it on?

Gilly lifted the hanger in her right hand. The sheath dress, with its smart little matching jacket, shimmered expensively in the still air. She lifted the hanger in her left hand.

Better play safe, perhaps.

Stick with the brown.

7
Oh, bugger!

Oh, *bugger!* Tory did keep from coming out with it, but still the word seemed to echo round the tinny little car as, finally, it spluttered to a halt. Mrs Collett said nothing either, (though her silence was more versatile somehow, redolent equally of criticism of the absent George, disdain for Tory's choice of family vehicle, and weary satisfaction at a calamitous prediction come true). In the mirror, Tory could see Gilly already shrinking, chameleon-like, into the cheap upholstery. As usual, then, it was up to her to sort the family out. Tory got out of the car, barely resisting the urge to batter it. What was wrong with the sodding thing *now?* Tory trawled through some half-remembered gleanings from the car maintenance course she'd taken years ago (presumably to make some point at George, since she could remember practically nothing). Clogged air filter? Blockage in the carburettor? Out of petrol? Oh, for heaven's sake! Not even George would dare do *that* to her on Barbara's wedding day.

No point in delving under the bonnet, anyway. That much she knew. All she would manage would be to smear oil on her best green frock, or, worse, the borrowed hat. No way round this one. She was going to have to phone Andrew Taylor at the Esso garage. Only a man on whom her family had some kind of psychic hold could be prevailed upon to rescue them on a Saturday morning.

Between the bend on which the car had stopped and

the one house in sight, there was a muddy track. Oh, God! Her suede shoes. Tory took them off, and then, ignoring both her mother's trenchant lack of comment and Gilly's look of panic, she peeled her tights off too. Still without any of the three of them having uttered a word, Tory set off between the flat expanses of field, barefoot over the patterned corrugations of tractor tyres pressed into mud.

And had a vision. An extraordinary thing. The hardening rippled pleats pressed up against the soft soles of her feet, and she was there again, at Tadley Beach, set to watch over Gilly as they paddled – this way as far as the ice-cream sign and no further; then back again, only as far as the Ladies into which Mother had stepped, just for a moment, to peel off the clinging wet bathing costume in which she fully expected to freeze to death.

And Gilly disappeared. One minute the world was rolling on its rightful way, sunlight glinting on waves, a cool hard rippling of sand underfoot, and cold, cold splashed ankles. And the next, Gilly was gone. Instantly, the world drained of colour. In some extraordinary parody of going blind, a sickly light bleached over everything, making it hard to see. The seagull overhead let out one last heart-rending cry, and time stopped utterly. Victoria stood alone: alone on her stretch of beach; alone in the world; alone in the hard-faced universe.

The fingers gripped her arm like claws.

'Where is your sister? Where *is* she?'

Tory fought desperately for breath and sense.

'She's –'

'*Tell* me!'

'She's –'

And there she was. The world came right again as, in a happy avalanche of spinning stones, Gilly slid down the cliff behind.

'There!' cried Victoria. And in the rush of her reprieve, she lost her head entirely. 'I knew where she was all along. I was just teasing.'

The slap sent her flying, spilling her into shallows on puckered sand. The fright of that lasted only for seconds. But, oh, the length of all the days afterwards. Her mother's grim refusal to smile, to speak, give any response at all. The cold, cold shoulder. Mealtimes, and passing on the stairs, encounters in the garden. And not a word. Just that mechanical jerk of the cheek to left, or right, whenever Tory came near. Left. Right. Left. Right. The freeze went on so long that Tory even learned to still her thumping heart, making a gamble of it. Left? Or right? Which way would the head turn? Get it correct three times in a row, and maybe forgiveness would follow.

Would it hell?

Left, right. At least the farmhouse had a telephone. Left, right. Tory marched closer. If Andrew was working this morning, if he came at once, if it was something simple he could fix, the three of them still might manage to slink in the chapel before the wedding was over. (They could make up for it afterwards by getting to the reception first, while Barbara's vans got lost.) Left, right. There was a woman standing on the step, watching her striding closer. Left, right. Left, right.

'Excuse me, may I borrow your telephone? I've had a bit of trouble with my car.'

8

The ring on her finger

After the wedding, the vans got lost promptly, as they always did. *Turn RIGHT straight after the common* Barbara had written in huge letters on the instructions with the map. But Bunster and Dido were busy arguing whether the priest had been unreasonable about the ramps, and didn't notice till too late. By then, they had got themselves entangled on the slip-road, and had to go on to Rippley before they could turn back.

Howard and Ellie did better. They got as far as Great Furley before Ellie said 'Down here, Howard!' with such authority that he turned up a side road of such poor construction that it could (and did) only lead to a farmyard.

The patients were stoical. (Only the wheelchairs in the front afforded any view.) The four in the back chatted among themselves. 'Never mind.' 'Soon find ourselves.' 'Give Barbara more time to get organized.' 'What a nice man she's married!'

For Miguel-Angel had been good to them. At Barbara's suggestion, he'd arrived early at the chapel and gone round shaking hands, and patting shoulders, and saying a few words to everyone. 'As charming as the Princess,' they'd all agreed (experienced recipients of kindness), and kept their wheelchairs as quiet as possible while he and Barbara took their lifelong vows. *'With this ring, I thee wed; with my body, I thee worship; with all my worldly goods, I thee endow.'*

'A bit old-fashioned,' complained Ellie, but everyone despised her for saying it, and thought her simply jealous. Phil (whom she had finally landed just a month ago) wasn't a patch on glorious Miguel-Angel who, dressed in white, stood waiting at the altar with such presence that many of them had been quite mesmerized out of the usual run of twitch and flap. The chapel was almost quiet through the ceremony. And, married at last to their beloved Barbara, he'd turned with a look of such triumph he'd almost given them permission to cough and jerk and quaver, letting loose their pent-up feelings.

Three rows behind, the man who drove Barbara's brother to the chapel sat, stood and kneeled, po-faced, through it all. The seats between, that had specifically been left for Barbara's mother and sisters and their families, stayed empty throughout. But when the groom turned to his mother and father on the other side, he showed no sign of irritation or distress. Neither did Barbara.

'And now you're mine,' he said to her softly as he handed her between the wheelchairs and smiles and greetings.

'Yes,' she said gratefully.

She'd reached the door before her mother and her sisters came hurrying up the steps.

'Are we too late? Oh, no, dear! I did think you might hold it for a little while.'

Miguel-Angel stepped forward, pulling the heavy gold fobwatch out from his breast pocket.

'Two o'clock,' he said, shaking his head in simulated regret. 'Busy again here at three.'

It manifestly wasn't true. (The priest had joined Caspar and the helpers for a cigarette.) But Mrs Collett didn't argue. She kissed the bride, and shook Miguel-Angel's parents' hands, and made as much as she could of the sheer undependability of small French cars without offending Tory, who was well within earshot and embarrassed enough.

'Good thing we didn't lash out on new outfits,' Gillyflower tried to comfort her sister.

Tory glanced round at all the other guests.

'I feel quite overdressed.' There was, she thought, some excuse for the ones in the wheelchairs. Shopping for clothes was difficult enough. But the helpers could surely have made a bit more of an effort. Bunster and Dido looked frightful. Phil's jeans were patched, and Ellie didn't even look clean. Only the finance officer – what was his name? Howard? – had bothered to put on a suit.

And they were all smoking.

'Who's coming in the big van?' Bunster asked generally. 'The quicker we get there, the quicker they open the champagne.'

A few of Barbara's favourites wheeled themselves nearer the ramp.

'We can take two,' said Barbara. 'But only if your chair folds properly. No soldered jobs, I'm afraid.'

Only two qualifiers could be found. Barbara and Miguel-Angel took those, and Caspar, with his very much larger boot, took two of the soldered jobs, and their owners.

'Everyone else with me and Ellie,' Howard ordered. He turned to Barbara and Miguel-Angel. 'Shall we just follow you?'

'I have a map,' said Barbara. To her new husband's astonishment, she pulled it out of her bra. 'Don't forget to turn right straight after the common. If you miss that, you'll end up on the slip-road, and have to keep on to Rippley.'

'Right ho,' said Howard.

Miguel-Angel spoke rattlesnake fast to his father.

'What was that?' Barbara asked.

Mr Lopez de Rego spoke rattlesnake fast back.

'I don't understand a word.'

'He follows in his car.'

He took her hand and spun her round to face him. Taking her chin between his fingers, he looked into her eyes.

'Don't lose my parents,' he warned her. 'Drive very slowly.'

The ring on her finger felt strange against the steering wheel. She couldn't concentrate for happiness. He had to keep reminding her to use her indicators all the way.

9

Pinching the sunny spots

William couldn't help it. Call him putty-hearted, but he was moved by the way Caspar coped with their two unexpected passengers.

'Have you been at the unit long?' he'd started up, even before pulling the car out into the traffic that streamed past Fellaham Hospital. The young man Bunster and Dido had shovelled in the back had looked, frankly, so dazed and enfeebled that William wasn't surprised to hear no response at all from directly behind him. But the other one, the one who shook horribly, was clearly keen to keep his end up. He answered for both; and William listened, speechless but frightfully impressed, as Caspar easily and imperceptibly shifted the conversation from idle chat about the new unit buildings and their facilities, through general talk about specific treatments, to quite intimate details of both their medical histories. All this kept things rolling nicely through leafy and sun-speckled lanes. And by the time Caspar drew to a gentler halt than usual in front of the Partridge, William felt almost at ease.

Then apprehension returned. For Caspar, denizen of fast back roads, had got ahead of Barbara. How were they going to manage now?

But Caspar, again, proved equal to the task. He stepped out of the car and lifted the wheelchairs from the boot.

'Which one is yours?' he asked the chatty fellow, surprising William, to whom it had never occurred that a wheelchair might be as personal an appurtenance as trousers, or a pair of spectacles.

The chatty one grimaced towards the more battle-scarred of the contraptions.

Caspar brought it closer and snapped on the brake, impressing William again.

'Can you help me?'

Before he realized Caspar wasn't speaking to him, William had already sprung forward. To cover his embarrassment, he tugged at the front car seat as though that had been his intention in the first place, pulling free the torn sheet of plastic-coated litter that was jamming the slide rails, and shoving it tidily away in his pocket. When he looked up, it was to see the chatty one shaking his head even more violently than before.

'Swing and tip, we do usually.'

It was a foreign language to William. But Caspar seemed to understand. Sliding his hands under the pitifully atrophied and trembling knees, he swung the man round till his legs dangled over the gravel. Then he hauled the chair closer, taking particular care to arrange it so, even when suddenly filled, it wouldn't tip back and scrape his paintwork.

He leaned forward with both arms, as if to cuddle a large child.

'Ready, Bob? Count of three.'

When Caspar gathered him, Bob fell with all the resolution of dead weight into his arms. Swivelling him manfully on his twisted feet, Caspar tipped him into the wheelchair.

'Hope you've got a strong back,' Bob muttered in a tone that left even inexperienced William in no doubt that this was some nicety spoken only to mask the discomfort of his physical jarring.

'Don't you worry about me,' said Caspar – clearly the stock response. He bent to pick up Bob's dangling feet, and tucked them away on the tin ledge, causing William to realize, to his chagrin, that left to himself he would have released the brake and pushed off merrily, running Bob over his own feet.

Mortified, William said to Caspar, 'I'll do the other one, shall I?' and realized instantly he'd put his foot in it. The other had a name as well, and, during the journey, first Bob, then Caspar, had used it.

Caspar pretended William had meant the wheelchair.

'Yes,' he said. 'Let down the brake.' Then he warned the crooked bag of bones slumped in the other seat, 'Ready, Otto?' Without waiting for an answer, he scooped him up and round. William hurried forward with the wheelchair, and Caspar let Otto down. There were no mannerly exchanges this time. Otto's head swung to the side. Caspar put it straight again, slid out a headguard that William hadn't even noticed, and buckled two sets of straps firmly.

'Is that right?' he asked the totally unresponsive Otto.

William waited for Bob to answer on his companion's behalf. But then he realized there was an etiquette about this business as yet beyond him. For Bob said nothing, and after a few seconds Otto managed to gather parts of himself together sufficiently to make a sort of gesture of consent with some of the muscles still partially working in his distended face.

Only then did Bob speak up.

'He has a cushion, too.'

Caspar found it lying at the back of the boot.

'It goes behind him.'

Caspar put it there.

'Right?' he said, locking the car. 'Are we all set? Who's for whipping round the back garden and pinching the sunny spots before the others get here?'

Caspar and William pushed the wheelchairs past the huge piles of bricks stacked neatly along the side wall of the Partridge. The wicket gate proved a dire obstacle, till Caspar thought to kick one of its stanchions back. The patio steps were unhelpfully jagged. And the designer of the pebble-lined walk deserved to be boiled in oil.

'All right?' Caspar said to William when he caught up at last.

'All right,' panted William, though he was practically fit to drop. One thing had risen, though. His opinion of Caspar. That had shot up sky-high. As for his sister, who'd done this day in and day out for years – no way round this one, she must be a *saint*.

IO

Change of Land Use

Tory and Gillyflower lurked in the darkest corner of the entrance hall. Tory was inspecting the Partridge's nicely framed copy of the Licensed Premises Act 1968, while Gillyflower stared round, anxiously twisting the sash ties of her brown floral frock into outlandish knots.

'Should we go into the bar?'

'Where we'll be safer, do you mean?'

Gillyflower flushed.

'I suppose you're right. We have to go out there and face them all some time.'

'I don't see why,' Tory said sourly. 'After all, Mother's wriggled out of it.'

And it was true. With breathtaking breeziness, Mrs Collett had slipped back next door – 'Just for a moment, dears, to powder my nose and fetch my present' – and failed to come back again.

Gilly moved close enough to whisper to her sister.

'A fat little man on the staircase is watching us.'

Instantly, Tory turned to look. The way she did it was so obvious, so utterly uncompromising, that Señor Lopez de Rego felt no compunction about bowing affably in their direction. As a skilled hotelier, not to mention the father of the groom, he felt a responsibility towards these two skulking ladies. It had been discourteous of them to be late for the wedding. That had displeased him and outraged his precious Rosina. But life was too short to make enemies in a family to which one was now irrevocably linked. So Señor Lopez de Rego came over and took each lady's hand in turn.

'You must allow me to furnish you with a drink. Today we are toasting your sister and my son.'

Gilly's astonishment showed. And even Tory caught her breath, realizing how close she'd just sailed to unpardonable rudeness. As she and her sister were ushered out into brilliant sunlight, she wondered why neither of them had recognized him. He was, after all, dressed up to the nines, and, now she thought about it, he and his wife had been walking out of the chapel arm in arm when, thanks to the inspired intervention of Andrew Taylor, her hamstrung Consumer Choice for the Year in the Small Car had finally limped through the gates of the hospital. Maybe it was because, for all their shared careful speech and old-world courtesy, Mr Lopez de Rego didn't in the slightest resemble Miguel-Angel. Short and rotund, there was something distinctly unpolished looking about the sun-wrinkled face that now turned again in her direction, and the stubby worn fingers that pressed a glass of champagne in her hand.

Not that there was anything the slightest unpolished about the diamond that flashed in his tie-pin.

'Thank you,' said Tory, cowed by his excellent manners into showing her own.

'Your English is wonderful,' said Gilly, in giggles even before she'd taken a sip from her own sun-sparkling glass. 'Where did you learn it?'

'Like my son,' Señor Lopez de Rego said proudly, 'I learned it here in the mother country. Brown's. Rules. The Ritz.'

'The *Ritz*?'

Now Gilly *was* impressed. But Mr Lopez de Rego had already turned to draw his wife away from the little clutch of wheelchairs at her side into the conversation.

'Rosina, I must introduce you.'

He spread out his hands to each sister.

'Victoria,' said Tory.

'Gillian,' said Gillyflower. 'Don't you think it's the most *wonderful* weather for a wedding?'

'Where is your mother?' Rosina asked, still only halfway thawed.

Since Tory never lied, this one fell naturally to Gillyflower.

'I'm sure she'll be back in a moment. She just had to nip next door to do one or two small things.'

'Next door?'

Gilly decided to leave this one to Tory, whose explanation that their mother lived over the wall led, inexplicably, to quite a detailed conversation about the precise nature of the boundaries between the two properties. In so far as Gilly could follow, either Mr Lopez de Rego's English was nowhere near as good as she had thought, or he was of the very odd opinion that the wall was no longer of any actual relevance. Since Tory was constitutionally incapable of abandoning any argument, no matter how pointless or ill-conceived, the discussion had very soon gone on far longer than poor Gilly could bear. And since Rosina Lopez de Rego had, in any case, turned her attention back to her previous conversation, Gilly decided it was perfectly polite to get away herself. The route past Rosina was firmly blocked by wheelchairs; but by sliding carefully backwards between the magnolia and the purple buddleia, Gilly managed to reach the path that led back to the veranda.

William was standing at the top of the steps.

'Who's that man over there?' he demanded of his sister, the moment she stepped within earshot.

'Which man?'

'That fellow with the ghastly orange hair.'

Gillyflower peered.

'Why, that's Dougie, of course.'

'I thought as much! And what's *he* doing here?'

'I expect Barbara invited him.'

'But *why?*'

Gillyflower stared at her brother.

'Why shouldn't she invite him? He's a *cousin.*'

'For Christ's sake!' said William, and promptly disappeared through the nearest hole in the yew hedge. Behind it, he found a man he was convinced he knew, peeing discreetly on the winter jasmine. When the man zipped up and turned to face him, it became obvious that it was Andrew Taylor from the Esso garage.

'What are you doing here?'

'Just checking up on Tory's car. It's had a bit of a problem.'

'Well, you'd better not start checking on Barbara,' William said sternly. 'You missed your chance at that four years ago.'

'Didn't I just?' said Andrew wistfully. And William couldn't help but follow his gaze. Under the shadow of the massive sycamore, Barbara was leaning against the back of a stone bench, an elegant cream lily hemmed in by proud patients in wheelchairs, waiters in full glorious tog, and colleagues and friends happily raising their glasses. Even as they watched, Mrs Lopez de Rego dropped her droopy wide-brimmed white sun hat on to her new daughter-in-law's head in an impromptu gesture of affection, and Barbara tipped it fetchingly to the side. She looked enchanting. She looked radiant.

Andrew broke into William's reverie by asking suddenly,

'Who are those chaps over there?'

'Which chaps?'

'That gang near the balustrade.'

Now it was William's turn to peer across the flock of guests.

'They're just some friends of Barbara's.'

'Funny friends!' Andrew Taylor snorted, before calling to mind the nature of present company. 'Oh, sorry, Will!'

But William, so used to this sort of thing he barely noticed, still took the chance to melt away. He wandered off towards the potting shed, thinking about love and Barbara, and then about Caspar and purple rhododendrons. They'd had some gala couplings down this little path, and, notwithstanding the nightmare presence on this day of days of ghastly Dougie Macpherson, William felt his spirits rise. What a fine soul Caspar had proved himself to be over the last few weeks. He'd paid for the whole of Barbara's wedding, bugger the price, and even forced William into getting this silly new suit, in which he admitted he looked thoroughly dashing. The fellow deserved a good treat. Definitely. What William ought to do was slip across the wall, and while his mother was still lurking (inveterate party truant) in the house, he'd creep through the unlocked door and up the back stairs, and pick something from the dressing-up bag. Hector's old naval uniform, perhaps? And maybe that primrose yellow silk-lined tricornered hat.

William put his foot on a knot in the sycamore's vast trunk, and hauled himself up and over. There was a moment on the other side when he feared for the safety of his new suit. But one firm push outwards kept him clear of the wall. He grazed his fingers, though. And it was while he was searching his pockets for a scrap of tissue to wipe off the blood that he came across the torn sheet of paper he'd pulled out from under Caspar's passenger-seat slide rail.

Even with the protective coating peeled away, the paper wasn't much use. William dabbed at his fingers, but it didn't absorb. The blood just smeared across the line of type – *planning permission to build seven chalet-sty* – and down through – *nd address of landown* – to – *th Co* – beneath.

th Co?

Lilith Collett?

William looked up and saw the pegs. Like goblin telegraph poles poked up from hell, they marched the whole way across the garden. Even through rising tremors of rage, the thought did cross his mind that, if his mother had only had the charity to let a few things flourish, no one would even have noticed them. But on this barren turf, they were unmissable. William strode up the line, a towering Brobdingnagian of wrath. Under a harshly pruned stump beside the last peg, he found a balled-up sheet of paperwork dropped by the surveyor. *Item 7: Change of Land Use – subdivision of rear garden, Cold Domain, Little Furley*, and, in ball-point underneath the tell-tale outline map: *authorized*, a scribbled signature – *W.D. Hamill, Councillor*, and last Wednesday's date. He tore the two pieces of official mischief into tiny shreds, hurling them up the garden like blossom in storm. Mother and

Caspar. Caspar and Mother. A joint betrayal. Double treachery. Blinded by tears, he staggered off, as if by instinct, towards the one corner of the garden where, for a few short unpruned summer weeks, a wounded creature might lie in covert green and tangled privacy, waiting for grief to triumph and heart to break.

And it was here that Joshua and the gang found him.

'I *knew* it was sobbing,' said Joshua, exhibiting infinitely more pleasure at being proved right than concern for the victim of misery.

'Is he sick?' Flora suggested.

'Sick people don't cry,' said Frou-Frou. 'He's just upset.'

'*Upset?*' said Joshua. 'A man doesn't cry like that when he's *upset.*'

The boy they'd picked up on the bypass, travelling south, just looked away. He'd felt like crying like that, only that morning, when the lorry driver from Bolton had finished with him. That's why he'd been so pathetically grateful when the peculiar little caravan had pulled up in the lay-by, and these two long-legged West Indian beauties had reached down to pull him inside.

'You're ours now.'

'And if you're not good, we'll feed you to Joshua.'

Joshua, still concentrating very much on getting back in lane, had merely muttered to his driving mirror:

'Keeping pets now, are we, girlies?'

And it had felt nice that way. Coddled and safe, like back at home but without his horrid parents. So when they'd told him, 'We're turning off at the next exit. Shouldn't we drop you?' he'd simply shaken his head.

Flora had shrugged.

'Come along if you want to, then.' She'd raised her voice to reach Joshua.

'Can he come?'

'Why not?' Joshua called back over the rattle of the loose seat. 'See if my Dad knows which one of us is his son.'

So here he was. With them, but expendable. With the result that when Joshua got impatient with the sobbing corpse, fastidiously tipping it back over on to its ugly, swollen face with his foot, it was him they left standing guard while they went off together to ruin the afternoon for Caspar in the most time-honoured and traditional manner: asking for free medical advice at a party.

The boy fancied himself as much as the next man as a soothing and sympathetic confidant.

'So what's the matter, then?'

William continued to snuffle horribly.

'What's up?' the boy persisted. 'Has someone died?'

It was so nearly true that William could scarcely bring himself to shake his head.

'Have you split up with someone?'

Behind his hands, William shuddered. That was a horror yet to come.

'Somebody hurt you?'

Was it the lick of feeling in the boy's voice? (The bruises, after all, were still warm on his bottom.) Certainly something triggered William's distraught attention. He opened his eyes. Before him, the vision of beauty that had brought Caspar screeching to a halt on the slip-road made William catch his breath.

'Oh, boy!'

After, neither was sure which of them started it. It

could have been the boy, running a finger experimentally down William's cheek, as if to check the tears were real. It could have been William, leaning forward to snatch the soft hand with its pale workshy fingers, and press it to more urgent business. Either way, over and over they rolled, out from the dark of the laurels on to the sunlit borders and back again, flattening gentians and speedwells and even the rare alpine campions that William had brought back from holiday in Cyprus. First sight of the boy's bruises drove William into frenzy, and the force of him set the boy squeaking. Their rocking, crashing jumble of desires snapped off the head of phlox and uprooted the saxifrage. Branches of laurel splintered, skewering soft flesh, and the scent of crushed leaves formed a bitter wall round them.

'Over', grunted William. And, again and again, '*Now*.'

At last, though, the boy had had enough. Pushing off his attacker, he keeled over on to his back, and stared up through the canopy of dark glossy leaves, panting his way back to common sense.

And William, too, surrendered to the fear of discovery.

'For God's sake! Get your clothes on!'

You had to hand it to him, William thought. He did what he was told. He didn't argue. And settled in the crook of William's arm, he lay so peaceably that gratitude speedily gave way to suspicion. Did the little tramp do this every day for a living?

What did it matter, though? He'd given William one hell of a boost. First time in the garden, too, since Dougie Macpherson. A pity the flame-topped creep over the wall didn't realize his ghost was finally, utterly, laid. (William 3 – or was it 4? – Herod the King 0.) But he'd be too busy to care, sprawled on his wrought-iron chair, swilling the champagne Caspar was paying for just as fast as he could gather the bottles around him . . .

But the resentment wouldn't take. William couldn't put his heart in it. It didn't seem to matter any longer.

Gently disengaging himself from the head lolling on his shoulder, he raised himself on an elbow to look around. My God! The damage they'd done in less than twenty minutes. Well, never mind. At least he'd managed to flatten memory along with the herbaceous border. And the boy seemed satisfied. He was snoring away quite merrily. Good idea.

William lay back and shut his eyes. Freckles of sunlight played on his eyelids through the leaves, and, spreading his hands, he felt an unaccustomed tingling in his fingers. He had forgotten how it felt to be relaxed, to let limbs lie heavy, and tired muscles sag. He hadn't lain like this for months and months and months. Not since the last time that they went abroad, and Caspar –

Caspar! Reminded, he tensed, waiting for anger to build, feeling to spark – anything. But nothing happened, and, for once, he couldn't bring himself to manufacture it. Somehow none of it seemed to matter any more. It was as if the imminent destruction of Cold Domain had pulled some giant plug in his own soul. His passion for the place had drained away, leaving him empty, bone dry. As clearly as if he'd given the words speech, he suddenly heard himself thinking, 'Oh, what does it matter, for God's sake? It's only a garden.'

Only a garden. Rasp of leaves. Breath of flowers. Flurry of birdsong. And the shimmer of air on his face. Only a garden. The tears rolled steadily down William's cheeks, but this time all the sorrow and regret was for himself. He suddenly saw, with bitter clarity, that, for the best part of the last thirty years, the ground lying under him might just as well have been pressing down on top, trying to suffocate him, a hateful dark shadow robbing his childhood and youth of all sunlight. He'd spent his whole bloody life worrying about this garden. What was she cutting down now? What was she ripping out this week? And now, in spite of all that, it was doomed. The giant digger sitting discreetly behind the Partridge's storeroom would move in any time it chose. But for the wedding, it probably would have started its evil work early on Thursday morning. The turn of a key, a spit of diesel and a penetrating roar, and years of his love, devotion and concern would be ground up in its steel maw.

And, still, it didn't matter. William scoured every corner of his soul, but still his whole regret was for himself. About the garden, he no longer cared. Not any more. Not now he realized he'd misspent his life. Like someone who stepped out in evening air after an opera, and felt whipped-up passion suddenly subside, and spurred emotion shrivel, William looked back and saw his whole life for what it was. A horrible mistake. A lost cause. Wasted time. What was it Barbara had said? 'You and I just go on and on about everything to do with Cold Domain. But it's a bad habit, and there isn't any point. We're not children any longer, and I'm stopping.'

William took a deep breath.

'Right,' he said sternly and out loud. 'I'm stopping too.'

Beside him, the boy stirred. His pretty head rolled closer to a jagged root, so William protectively scooped it back on his arm. Then, feeling more at peace than he could remember, he fell in such a dreamless sleep that even the noise of Joshua and one of the girls crashing their way back through the undergrowth a few minutes later, laden with party drinks, failed to awaken him.

Flora looked down at the intertwined snorers.

'Babes in the wood,' she said. 'How *sweet*.'

But Joshua wasn't so sure. He'd had a funny feeling about the boy right from the start, for all that he'd gone to such trouble to flirt with both Flora and Frou-Frou. And, as for the other one, for all Joshua knew, he could be his father's special friend. After all, the quite extraordinary expression on Caspar's face while Frou-Frou was trying to explain what was presumably a run-of-the-mill anxiety of pregnancy had suggested to Joshua that his father might be in terror lest – what was the fellow's name? William? – sprang out from nowhere and introduced himself.

He prodded both the sleepers awake with his foot.

'Here,' he said, handing the boy one of the glasses he was carrying. 'Come alive, and join the party.'

He offered the other the quite extraordinary-looking cocktail the handsome Spaniard had given him.

'Are you William?' he asked suspiciously.

William sat up.

'Is that a Moosewood Tailwagger?' Gratefully, he seized it. 'Did Caspar send you to fetch me?'

'No,' Joshua said sourly. 'Caspar's busy.'

Now it was William's turn to be suspicious.

'Maybe we'd better get back.'

Flora was keen.

'It looked like a pretty good party,' she admitted wistfully. 'They were just starting wheelchair races on the lawn.'

Braced by the Moosewood Tailwagger, William sprang to his feet.

'Are you friends of Barbara's?' he asked the three of them civilly.

'No,' Joshua said. 'We were directed here by someone called Broadfoot.'

'Broadhurst,' William corrected.

'Broadbent,' said Flora.

She reached down to tug the dazed boy to his feet, and together the four of them walked back across the garden, past the line of pegs, to the huge sycamore, where William pointed out which of the holes in the wall furnished the best way of clambering over.

Flora went first. And then the boy.

'You're Joshua, aren't you?' William took the opportunity to ask, as, standing directly in startled Mrs Collett's line of sight, they waited their turn to climb over. 'How do you do?'

Joshua could hardly ignore the proffered hand, but that didn't mean he had to be overly civil.

'I'll be better when all this is over,' he said grimly.

Boxed soaps

Up in the bedroom, Mrs Collett dropped the fold of the curtain back in place. She'd be better when all this was over. It was unnerving, catching sight of her son shaking hands with a stranger in her garden. Had the two of them sprung out of the bushes? And what had they been doing there, for heaven's sake? Surely they would have introduced themselves to one another *first* . . .

Stop it! she told herself firmly. Stop it! Don't even think about it. Just get on.

She turned back to the clutter of boxed soaps on the bed. All this could go to Oxfam, with the rest. No room in her bungalow for boxed soaps and silly sets of matching towels. She'd give the lot away. What had she wanted with all this stuff anyway? Why had she kept it down the years? Barbara could come and take her pick, and all the rest was going. Out, out, out. She'd go and tell Barbara now, otherwise the happy couple might slip away, and, by the time the honeymoon was over, it could be too late. She might be out of here, safe in her little bungalow, where no one could touch her. The house was already on the market, and the first serious inquirer (foreign, of course) was apparently making much of the possibility of 'immediate entry'. But that would be all for the best, of course. No time to worry about anything. Pick what she wanted, and leave all the rest.

Snatching up a gift set of matching toilet seat cover and

mat, Mrs Collett made for the door. She'd leave the damned coffee percolator for later. It was too heavy to carry anyway. If either of her good-for-nothing sons-in-law had bothered to show up, she could have sent one of them back to fetch it. But Angus and George, of course, had made their excuses as usual. She hardly remembered what either of them looked like. Strange, wasn't it, how it could take a woman a whole lifetime to learn the tricks a man knew naturally?

She wouldn't bother, either, to latch the door. Let anyone who chose stroll in and take what they fancied. Less work for her.

Lilith flew out of the house so fast, she might have been on wings. Hurrying next door, clutching her box, she graciously took a cocktail from a young man in a wheelchair whose rather stiff and curious way of holding it led her mistakenly to believe that it was being offered, and set off on her first-ever tour of the Partridge, in search of Barbara and Miguel-Angel.

12

Wishes come true

Miguel-Angel leaned back against the door, blocking Barbara's way out.

'No, really,' she insisted, trying to look stern. 'We shouldn't creep away like this. We ought to go back, just for a little while longer.' Through champagne befuddlement, she played what she clearly thought was a masterstroke. 'Your parents might think that we're being rude.'

He grinned. (He'd had a lot more to drink than she had.)

'My parents owe me six months, not half an hour.'

Barbara only latched on to the last part.

'Half an hour!' She was shocked. Then she dissolved back into giggles. 'People will think we're –'

She couldn't think how to put it.

'Yes?'

She still couldn't think how to put it. She was about to sink down on the bed to mull it over when she realized he wasn't, as she'd assumed, patting the coverlet straight for her. He was tugging the whole thing across the bare floorboards.

'Door lock's broken,' he explained through gritted teeth.

'You're making dreadful marks on the floor.'

He seemed indifferent. She wondered if he was a bit too drunk to worry about keeping his job any longer. Not that the new owners of the Partridge wouldn't make allowances. Even their casual foreign bar staff couldn't get married every day. But still, the scratches on the floor-boards did look frightful. It was a very cheap tin bed.

Once it was safely jammed against the door, he turned his attention to the untidy pile of shining, beribboned boxes which had been carried upstairs only a few minutes earlier, when Señor Lopez de Rego, much taken with the first of many Moosewood Tailwaggers, had suddenly chosen to clear the gift table on the veranda in order to facilitate speedier manufacture. Miguel-Angel studied the heap of wrapped presents for a moment or two, then pounced on the largest square box. He picked it up and shook it.

'Ha!'

For all her head was swimming, Barbara still tried to be sensible.

'You ought to look at the label.'

Miguel-Angel tore off the tiny card studded with wedding bells, and hurled it in her direction.

'*With every good wish from Gillian and Angus,*' she read aloud fondly, before looking up to see her beloved hauling huge clouds of downie from the wrappings. 'Why, that's the very one they won in the raffle at Horridges' Christmas Party! I was there!'

He wasn't listening. He came across to start on the hooks and buttons and zips he'd been quietly sizing up through thirteen long fittings.

'Stop it!' she said shyly, pushing at his fingers.

He grinned again.

'Too late for that.'

'We can't,' she insisted. 'This isn't the right time.' (Though she knew from the most precious wedding gift of all, Broadbent's little pink basal thermometer, that there was no truth at all in what she said. It was *exactly* the right time.)

Only half as a joke, he bent his head to tug at one end of a ribbon with his teeth.

'No, really . . .' she said, surrendering.

Nuzzling her lovely cleavage, he mimicked her.

'No, really . . .'

She shook with laughter and the dress fell off. She wouldn't have believed it. But there it lay, round her feet, a puffball of cream silk. He took her hand, and she stepped out of it, on to the downie.

And then he pulled her down. How could you concentrate, as wishes came true? The whole time he was kissing and caressing, her head was spinning for love. The ring glowed on her finger. *With this ring, I thee wed.* The force of his passion crushed the breath out of her. *With my body, I thee worship.* And when, after groaning in joyous, blazing consummation, he lifted his weight off her at last, his foot went straight through the box containing George's aunt's wind chimes from Dublin. *With all my worldly goods, I thee endow.*

He picked obediently among the torn wrappings and the splinters of cut glass.

'*From Victoria and the family,*' he read from the little recycled brown label. '*With all our love.*'

They fell in one another's arms again, though whether from passion or laughter, neither could tell. When both their hearts stopped thumping, he stood up and pulled out the top drawer of his dresser.

'Time to go.'

'Go? Go where?'

'Honeymoon, of course.'

'Honeymoon?'

He turned to stare in mystification more than equal to hers.

'What did you *think?*'

The blank expression on her face proved that she hadn't thought at all. He shook his head at her, amazed, then went back to rooting in the drawers of his dresser. Items long tucked away showered all over her. Sunglasses, golden cuff links, Spanish driving licence, credit cards . . .

Credit cards!

In the mirror in front of him, he caught the reflection of her continuing confusion.

'Listen,' he said, sitting down and taking her gently by the wrist. 'Only a fool buys a hotel without knowing how it works. Figures on paper lie. Bar talk knows better. My father is no fool and so, before we bought it, he sent me.'

'You *own* this place?'

And then he realized. She'd kissed a frog and found a royal mate. But so had he.

'You never *guessed?*'

'You never *said*.'

His irritation with the past months surfaced.

'I hate the lies!'

'Have I been *very* stupid?'

He kissed the ring on her finger.

'Blind with love,' he assured her kindly. 'But you must open your eyes now. Lots to see.'

He told her all about it down the stairs. Houses and hotels in Spain. Courtyards and swimming pools. Apartments and fast cars. And a whole host of aunts.

Her head was spinning again.

'But what about my passport?'

Stopping short in the hotel doorway, he pulled from his wallet the fruit of his hasty trawl round her little room at Fellaham, where, exiled by tradition from her sight, he'd changed into his white suit.

She felt quite faint.

Now he was signalling the taxi outside to draw closer.

'One minute,' he said, thrusting the airline tickets in her hand as he helped her on to the back seat, and scooped the creamy folds of dress in after her. 'One thing to settle, then we're off.'

While he was gone, the taxi driver eyed her appreciatively in his mirror.

'You're off abroad now, are you?'

Barbara panicked again.

'Oh, God! I can't travel in this!'

'Nonsense! You look a treat!' the driver assured her, adding as an afterthought just as her eyes fell on the very words, printed on the tickets in her hand: *'First class!'*

13

Twice round the portable toilets, and back to base

One Moosewood Tailwagger, and Mrs Collett was thrusting her matching lavatory seat cover and mat out of the way in a camellia. What did her daughter want with gift sets anyway? China, bedlinen, children – if Barbara had any sense at all, she'd never start with matching anything.

Lilith turned back to the chaos surrounding her. Was that *Bernard* over there, bossing everyone mightily? 'Run that heat again, please! Bunster and Dougie! *In* line, not *over* it!' She was almost certain she'd spotted Andrew Taylor from the filling station on the veranda when she arrived. Perhaps Lilith had it wrong, and it was matching sets of old seducers that brides like Barbara went in for nowadays.

Mrs Collett stared in her drink. What could possibly be in it? When she looked up again, it was to see Mr Lopez de Rego imperturbably threading his way towards her through helter-skelter wheelchairs. Was he coming to see what she'd stuffed in the camellias?

'My dear Mrs Collett! I am so glad to see you back again. One more little Moosewood Wagtailer?'

Gamely, she tried to defend herself.

'Oh, no. Truly, I couldn't. This first one's already gone straight to my head.'

Mr Lopez de Rego insisted.

'To please *me*, the bride's new father!'

Lilith cast round for rescue. No hope of any help from

Gillyflower. Needled as usual by Angus's defection, but made bolder than usual with champagne, she seemed to be relentlessly setting her cap at a small group of Barbara's dubious-looking male friends, two of whom were quite visibly edging towards the bushes. Where was Victoria? Slipped off home early, no doubt. (The twins were always such a good excuse.) And, to be fair, she must have been sweltering in that particular green frock, which, serving as it did for her March anniversary every year as well, was rather warmly lined. Desperately, Mrs Collett scoured the lawn. Who else was there? Caspar, of course, standing, as usual, a little apart from all the trouble he'd caused, quietly enjoying a cigarette.

Señor Lopez de Rego saw Mrs Collett's eye fall on the distinguished-looking man in the bow tie who was grinding out his cigarette in the soil of the flowerbed, and, under the influence, perhaps, of one too many of his own variations of his son's cocktail recipe, mistook the glint of hostility in her eye for a burgeoning of interest. Thinking the two of them fairly well matched in age, and, in so far as he could judge, background as well, he determined to do her the favour of introducing them, even though the man's name had temporarily escaped him.

'Mrs Collett, may I present to you my son's new business factor?'

Caspar's look of astonishment passed him by. The necessarily functional introduction had put him in mind of the huge bill his son had thrust in his hand before leaving for the airport, and he was digging in his pockets for his cheque-book. Expertly adding on the cost of all the extra Moosewood Tailwaggers, plus variations, Señor Lopez de Rego scribbled the result of his calculations on a gold-embossed bank slip, while Caspar and Lilith dutifully shook hands.

'There,' he said, tearing off the vellum strip and giving it to Caspar, 'I hope that straightens the accounts a bit.'

A mere glimpse at the figure in the little box sent Caspar into shock. Reprieved like this, out of the blue, from what he now realized would have meant instant and ignominious beggary, he stood mute with gratitude, which, true to form, Señor Lopez de Rego at once mistook for an unbusinesslike preoccupation with Mrs Collett's attractions.

The silence was broken by a tirade from Bernard.

'Really, we can't have all these people littering the lawn! Strap them in properly, *please*! Not that direction, Ellie! Howard! Mind out!'

A gentleman by instinct, Señor Lopez de Rego took advantage of the nearby collision of wheelchairs to melt away, and leave things between these two rather stiff and old-fashioned English people to take their natural course, in their own time.

Caspar and Lilith stood, speechless with embarrassment, as Bernard barked out orders for the first semi-final.

'Flora! Back Otto up a bit, so his foot falls out of that thorn bush! Rosina, are you ready to drop the hanky? Stop *pushing*, Joshua, please. And what is Frou-Frou doing in Bob's wheelchair? Where have you put Bob? Is he in the *hedge*?'

Things could have turned out worse, thought Mrs Collett. She might have had Bernard as a son-in-law.

'Well!' she said, finally and brightly. 'What's done is done. And I hope Barbara will be happy.'

'She's happy already,' Caspar pointed out.

The notion was such a strange one that Mrs Collett fell back on silence for a refuge.

'I can't really imagine it,' he heard her admitting to herself at last. 'I don't think I've ever been happy. Not ever.'

It was quite evident she wasn't speaking for effect. And, out of nowhere, he suddenly felt the urge to try and comfort her.

'I think it's probably genetic,' he said. 'Like red hair or short sight. Either you're born with it, or you're not.'

A vestige of professionalism shone through at the last moment.

'Though don't quote me on that, please.'

He needn't have worried. She could barely hear a word. Bernard was bellowing again.

'*Behind* the ramps, everyone! Right! Pay attention! Twice round the portable toilets, and back to base!'

Mrs Collett suppressed a shudder. Yes, things could definitely have turned out worse. Her eye swept the ranks of lunatics risking death or serious injury in the last of the semi-finals, and came unwittingly to rest on a long-legged black girl struggling with Dougie Macpherson for the occupancy of a battered wheelchair.

'Who is that pretty child in the beads and the black boots?'

Distinctly, she heard Caspar snort.

'That "child" goes by the name of "Frou-Frou". And she is four months pregnant. By my son!'

Clearly, his feelings on the subject were strong ones. But these days it was so easy to misinterpret other people's attitudes. Should she be sympathizing with him over having a black grandchild? Or over its fairly certain imminent miscarriage?

Picking her words very carefully, Mrs Collett asked:

'I wonder if you'd be happier if she sat out the next race?'

Caspar gave her a quick glance. He was surprised by the sensitivity of her response. Up till now, he'd taken the woman for an unabashed racist. But his reply, when it came, was fuelled by the fatalism of years of experience.

'Either she'll lose it, or she won't.'

The need to share his anxiety made him a little more communicative than usual.

'It seems, at my son's suggestion, she's only eating bright yellow foods at present, to try and endow the baby with her own sunny nature.'

Mrs Collett was shocked.

'Surely her own doctor has spoken to her quite sharply?'

Caspar sighed, and lit another cigarette.

'Apparently, Frou-Frou doesn't hold with doctors. The only reason she came looking for me is that the baby hasn't started kicking yet.'

'I'm not at all surprised,' said Mrs Collett, watching the race start with a ferocious clash of wheels. 'The poor mite! It's probably desperate for any peace and quiet it can get.'

Following Frou-Frou's turbulent progress across the lawn, she had a sudden feeling of despair about the world. Really, the parents to whom some poor unfortunates were born! It almost broke your heart. Hippies and cranks, gullible horoscope readers and members of mad religious sects. And those were just the fools. Inside the bran tub there were villains too. Murderers, sadists, drunks. You only had to read the papers for a week or two to see how lucky your own offspring had been. Like Caspar's Joshua, with his nice mushroom-carpeted flat, safe job in computers and nippy little hatchback, her four had all had a good start in life. And, like Caspar's Joshua, see how they mindlessly threw it over and let you down! Tory and Gillyflower had married men of cast-iron selfishness, and gone their own sweet way. Off on a honeymoon that might last weeks, Barbara had not even made the effort to come next door and say goodbye to her mother. And, as for William! The way he went on, nipping in and out of bushes with perfect strangers, didn't bear thinking about.

But at least, so far, he'd refrained from bringing home a black baby!

Poor Caspar. Poor, poor Caspar . . .

All feelings of bitterness towards him swept away, Lilith laid her hand comfortingly on her companion's arm.

'You must come round and see my lovely new bungalow,' she told him gently.

Now it was Caspar's turn barely to hear a word. Entirely taken up with willing his precious, precious grandchild to cling more tightly to its mother's womb, and so to life, he answered without thinking:

'That's awfully nice of you, Lilith. I'd enjoy that a lot.'

14
Finale

From the deep shadow of the sycamore, William watched his mother drop her hand on to Caspar's sleeve, and murmur in his ear. Caspar responded immediately, William noticed, though he was careful not to draw attention to their cosy little exchange by taking his eyes off the wheelchairs for a moment. It was impossible to guess what either of them was saying. But William saw that Señor Lopez de Rego, passing within earshot with a fresh tray of cocktails, could not resist darting a knowing smile across the lawn at his wife. Did everybody in the *world* know what was going on, except for him?

William shrank further back into shadow as a fresh spate of commandments from Bernard signalled the end of the race.

'Winners back into their positions, *please*! Dougie, you're *out*! Hurry up, everyone. Time for *il grand finale*!'

Rosina smiled sweetly, in deference to what she presumed was Bernard's brave stab at her language. Caspar and Lilith were forced apart as, noisily arguing tactics, the determined finalists clattered the last few wheelchairs with any life left in them back to the starting line. Caspar at once took off towards the hotel's back entrance. And everyone else stood round, or, in the case of the exhausted or the paralysed, were propped neatly against the sturdier shrubs in a row along the flowerbeds.

William took off after Caspar. Keeping well out of sight

in the thick greenery, he all but stepped on two of Barbara's funny friends, who were taking advantage of the fluffy matching toilet set they had found in the bushes to enjoy a much comfier, though still exotic, coupling. Through mutual murmured apologies, William backed off, getting halfway along the shadow of the balustrade before he was stopped short by Caspar's voice, above him on the veranda.

'No, really, I don't believe . . .'

'Of course we've met! You're Mr Hamill, from the Council. I recognized you instantly, though you've unsportingly shaved off that very fine moustache!'

William took Caspar's interlocutor for a madman. Then he heard Caspar say.

'Well, since you're here . . .'

William raised himself to peer through a gap in the wisteria. To his astonishment, it was the hotel's solicitor who had accosted Caspar. William was baffled by the man's quite uncharacteristic lack of grip. He hadn't been nearly so prone to confuse all the details the day he precipitately sacked William as a barman. (William could still remember, only too well, the sheer, unarguable precision of most of the accusations during that very unpleasant interview, and the even more meticulous threats that followed when William, on his way out, ill-advisedly raised the issue of financial compensation for dismissal without notice.)

Caspar, on the other hand, seemed to know perfectly well with whom he was dealing. Like a man cornered by the representative of some wholly worthy charity, he had already begun to fish in his jacket for his wallet. William lowered himself more comfortably on to the ground. He knew the waves of genteel murmuring that spilled from Caspar on the presentation of accounts. '. . . naturally happy to give you a percentage now, of course . . . a few days to check over the details at my leisure . . . in full at the end of the month . . .'

Was that a plain *rustle* he was hearing? William raised himself up again. Yes, it was true. Without a word of the usual procrastination or complaint, Caspar was handing a cheque to the hotel solicitor.

He wasn't even scowling.

'A quite enchanting wedding!' And then, mysteriously, 'Worth every peseta!'

The solicitor's bafflement turned to reverence when he inspected Caspar's offering.

'My word!'

And, equally awed, William dropped back into shadow. He'd seen the cheque as well, as clear as paint. And it was from no twopenny account, that was quite obvious. Vellum, and gold-embossed – like nothing he had ever seen before. What sort of day was this? His mother and his lover in cahoots. His garden sold. And the ensuing forty pieces of silver (money that could have launched his precious chain of restaurants) tucked in a secret bank account. How far could the poison spread from one betrayal? How deep a pit be dug for his last hopes?

William slunk off towards the table on which Señor Lopez de Rego had set up his little manufacturing process for Moosewood Tailwaggers, and variations. No limes were left. All of the Caribbean rum was gone. And a cigarette end floated in the last of the Triple Sec. Still, William did his best. There was an unwanted moment of civility when Frou-Frou, called sharply back to the starting line by Bernard halfway through squeezing herself a lemonade, insisted on hijacking his first lurid yellow apology for a real Tailwagger. But when, after only a couple of quick sips, a look of transfiguring happiness crossed her face, and she clutched at her stomach, he had the presence of mind to snatch it back.

Two more, and even the cascades of happy shrieking from the lawn could not distract him from his purpose. Above the noise, nobody heard the engine of the digger spurt to life. That William was a noticeably inexpert driver was born out by the regular suspensions of his licence. But this did give him the advantage of being less concerned than most with having very little idea at all which of the various pedals and levers were having what effect on his progress. (He didn't bother with the knobs at all.) The digger rumbled bronchially down the drive. It went so slowly, steering it was easy. And though the engine seemed to be putting far more of an effort than it need into the mild slope downhill from the Partridge, and the short trip next door, still William chose to leave the bulk of the controls exactly where he found them, until the narrowness of the lane outside his mother's gates forced a level of experiment and invention upon him.

He wouldn't call it quite a three-point turn. But, time-consuming and laborious as it was, it definitely worked on the same principle. Soon he was grinding merrily past the shrubbery. Where should he practise? On the old tennis court? Down what was once lavender walk? Or on the grass?

Why practise? Why not start directly up the line of pegs, and work his way across? As with so many of the skills he had acquired over the years – juggling, metal-work, cooking – he'd be bound to get better much quicker than expected. Probably he'd have the knack of it – lower the mechanical teeth, rip up a sizeable chunk of garden, toss it aside – before he got anywhere near the stretches skirting the dividing wall.

Not that he expected any of them to bother to raise their heads and glance over. Up until now, no one had even noticed his absence. He'd heard, 'Dougie, get back in line!' and, 'Rosina! The hanky!' often enough in the last hour or so. But not once had he heard any cries of 'Where's William?'

Stop it! he told himself. Stop it! Part of the resolution he'd just made was giving up self-pity. He had allowed the vile and snivelling habit to nurture and comfort him his whole life through, but he was finished with it. Stop. The *end*. It wasn't natural to him, anyway; just something he'd picked up inadvertently from his mother. Why, he could even remember stopping short on the landing one night on his way to the bathroom, on hearing a venomous hiss from behind his parents' door. 'Self-pity's the only pleasure that interests you now, isn't it, Lilith?' And Hector had been right. That cast-iron habit of always looking inward, never out, had even stopped her seeing others as they truly were, not how she chose to imagine them. 'I suspect Tory would secretly like another child, and it's only George stopping her.' 'It's my belief that William isn't half as "gay" as he thinks.' A strange way of going about life, to put half your considerable energies into a series of utterly false constructions, and the rest into forcing others to pretend to believe you. A massive, massive waste of effort and time, like those whole afternoons she'd been prepared to spend policing his swallowing of the last few mouthfuls of lunch. (Show him a plate of mackerel even now, and he would *heave*.) But was it true, what they said, about habits being first cobwebs, then cables? Surely, if he were strong, the real self could break through, even if it meant quelling the patterns of a lifetime. Surely, like any other mad charade, this one could end at will. He must have heard her say it a thousand times. 'You're like me, William. We're peas in a pod.' And he had simply smiled. What did she know about him? Not a thing. What was the point of arguing? But now, almost too late, he saw how close his idle complaisance had brought her to a total victory. Merely at the memory of the familiar claim, his fingers gripped the levers more tightly, and, as if he were ten years old again, back in the playground, he felt like screaming, 'It isn't true, so take it back! Take it back!'

Get a grip, William. Shoulders down. Breathe out slowly. Take your time. Remember, the vow was made. Like Barbara, he'd moved on. There were to be no more tears and panics, no more frantic moods. From this day on, he'd walk in the light of detachment, with soaring ecstasy and dragging pain no more than sweepings from his past – needed along the path, perhaps, but certainly not any longer. Nothing and nobody would ever tip him back into high feeling. He'd learned the value of indifference. At last – at long, long last – he had grown up. Something had gone, but, in return, he'd gained a quality of infinite value. He'd gained an incandescent inner peace.

The beatific smile persisted through the grinding crash of gears, the whine of rising speed, and then the thundering, earth-shaking fall of the mechanical steel jaw. His juddering excursion up the pegs left in its wake a bleeding brown stripe of earth. Down the ridges he was raising on both sides, his whole childhood was sliding. On this very grass he was filleting, he had learned first to walk, later to somersault, and then to turn a perfect string of cartwheels. On what were now dark saddles of ploughed soil, he'd lain for hour after hour, pretending to study for this examination, or for that, but really just waiting for one massive silver-edged cloud after another to sail in its stately fashion over the sycamore, releasing the sun, with its glorious, eye-filling rainbows, its power to infuse a blissful warmth through to the very bone. Here, where he swung the digger round, was the exact spot where, home from school to the news that his precious litter of kittens had gone to 'a good home', he'd thrown himself, blind with tears, on to the grass, and found the tell-tale damp ring of their bucket drowning. Here, where he ground his path of destruction past the laburnum, was where she'd thrashed him half-stupid simply for repeating a rumour about Mrs Philimore's drunken husband that he'd overheard from her in the first place. The garden was thicker with memories than it was with plants, but the whole lot were going. Out, out, out! The digger forced them up, and tossed them to the side. They wouldn't bother him again. Memories, like feelings, were to be extirpated from the new, reformed William. These stubborn ghosts were of no value, anyway. Everyone's early years were littered with frustrations and cruelties, and no cruelty or frustration seems petty to the victim. We are all Wednesday's children, deep at heart. Caspar was right. Most childhoods were barbaric. You only had to read the papers for a week or two to see how very lucky you had been. Half of the children in the world were born to families who scarcely fed and clothed them properly ('Forced you to finish your dinner? You were *lucky!*'). Look at the house where Caspar had grown up. My Christ! Caspar looked smooth enough, but what a dank hole that turned out to be. Even from where they stood at the corner of the alley, it was quite obvious that, out of the window to which Caspar pointed, you would see nothing but bricks. Who could compare one cradle curse with another? What was a childhood of bricks compared to his years of enchantment in this glorious garden?

Not that the place was looking all that glorious now. By God, the digger had done a quick and thorough job of chewing up Old Mother Nature's steady efforts. William twisted in the seat and peered back, over his shoulder. The desolation was astonishing. The garden was half-wrecked. You'd only know that this was Cold Domain because of the timeless and immovable sycamore.

The sycamore! For God's sake! How was he going to get past it this time round? The heaps of earth the digger had thrown up blocked the way on one side. His frenzied turns had made a steeper ridge than usual. It was a toss-up, to the inexperienced, whether the digger would trowel its way successfully over the mound, or whether it would grind to the top, and promptly topple over. He'd better stop the thing at once (though, in the horror of the moment, he couldn't even think how he'd originally switched it on).

'*William!*'

The pedal that, up till now, he'd taken for a sort of

brake, proved, when he stamped on it, dangerously feature-
less. The digger aimed directly at the tree.

'*William*! For God's *sake*!'

He hadn't the least idea which of the crowd of them
suddenly bellowing at him over the wall had a voice
strident – or desperate – enough to reach him. Or was
daft enough not to realize he wasn't facing hand-picked
options here. The only thing that he could do was *steer*
the bloody thing. Left, into the garage – *splat* – or
right, catapulting over a soil cliff and straight under the
wheels – *splat* – or into the trunk of the sycamore.
Splat!

What was the point of bothering to choose?

Under the very shadow of the tree, the life-force in
William stirred. The digger lurched so desperately to the
left that he was nearly hurled from the little bucket seat.
The garage doors split open like ripe fruit, and, as the
digger skewered its splintering timber shell, old tools of
Hector's, rusted over years, hurtled like shrapnel at the
line of onlookers, forcing them to duck behind the safety
of their rampart.

'*William*! The *brake*! For God's *sake*!'

He tried again, pulling knobs, slamming levers, and
jamming his feet as hard as he could against one pedal
after another. Ten yards of ancient wall keeled over in a
perfect surfer's wave, revealing those guests whose physical
condition precluded scrambling, first for a view of what
was going on, then, at this perilous moment, for escape.
William pulled something else, to which the only evident
response was that the monstrous steel jaw spitefully
dropped to a deeper, more critical angle, slowing the
digger almost to a halt against its still frantically straining

engine. Everyone stared as, through the air, a host of tiny coloured stones showered like confetti. The beautiful glittering fragments hung for a few long moments in the sky, then fell in scattered arcs of green and blue.

William flung back his head. Mesmerized, he watched the shimmering, spinning jewels tumble back down to earth. He didn't know much about what was hidden, layers deep, but he recognized history when he saw it. These tiny shards of mosaic tile must have been buried for centuries. On to him rained the past. Shattered. Destroyed. It was a sign. If something that had been buried as long as that could be uprooted with such ease, such speed, it was a sign that he, too, could begin again.

Exhausted, William slumped forward. It was over. His fingers loosened round the levers he'd been gripping to keep his balance on the shuddering machine. The engine's mad roar fell back to an idle cradling. William barely noticed Barbara's new father-in-law climb up beside him, or the soft tenor voice cheerfully carolling a foreign tune with foreign words as the stubby worn fingers pushed in a knob here, pulled back a lever there. The diggers on which this industrious Spaniard had made his first fortune (building hotels along unspoiled coasts) were slightly different in design, but nothing to hinder the resourceful. Some of the men who worked for him were positive maniacs. He'd had to sort out a lot worse. The boy had gone about the clearance in the most dementedly unsystematic fashion. (For a brief moment, Señor Lopez de Rego had even feared for the tree.) But, give him his due, he'd stayed on this side of the line of pegs, and the whole section was, in any case, destined for a clean sweep. The plans were extensive. The tiny, elegant chalets were to be almost hidden in a timeless, old-fashioned, run-riot secret garden. There'd be a rockery, rose-trellis walks, and maybe even that lovely stone fish tank Rosina had noticed under a heap of fireplace surrounds at Fellaham Architectural Salvage that morning, when they were killing time before the wedding. And there'd be climbers over everything. Climbers and creepers and lush, overgrown greenery. And lilacs. He absolutely loved soft-scented English lilacs. Barbara would help him plan it. All English-women were supposed to be brilliant at making gardens. He'd even ask her if she thought it might be possible to grow a vine inside the old greenhouse, once it had been restored. And what were those beautiful trees that ex-ploded in glorious blossom every summer? What were they called? No matter. Barbara would know. He'd plant a whole grove of them over there, where her brother had just torn out those very ugly tree stumps.

But time enough to think of all that later. Now he had better get the young man safely off the machine. All the excitement of his sister's wedding (and Miguel-Angel's splendid Moosewood Wagtailers) had clearly proved a shade too much for this particular reveller.

Señor Lopez de Rego waved cheerily to Caspar, who was already threading his way between the last of the guests outstaying their welcome round the breach in the wall, some on their feet, some in the wheelchairs, and some still propped in the flowerbeds. He watched him pick his way carefully across the freshly rutted terrain, paying attention to the ends of his trousers. The man was sensible enough. He'd sort the boy out, put him on his feet. And making the effort to take charge of the son could do nothing but good for his suit for the mother.

'Over to you,' Señor Lopez de Rego told Caspar.

Caspar looked up.

'William?' he prompted gently.

William looked down.

Years in the hotel trade had reinforced Señor Lopez de Rego's natural gift for keeping a neutral expression. Still, he was shocked by the fond way the older man reached up for the younger. And even more by the abandoned way William fell in his arms. Suspicion was bolstered by the way they failed to move apart. But, quite unwilling to mar the pleasure of his own son's wedding day with such unpleasant conjectures, Señor Lopez de Rego slid off the digger and went to give assistance to his wife, and Bunster and Dido, who were trying to match the more prostrate of Barbara's patients with the more functional of the remaining wheelchairs. A little bit of soldering here and there, and one or two of the battered metal carcasses lying around could probably be salvaged. Hadn't he seen a soldering iron fly through the air, and land in a holly bush? And was that soldering wire in that tree? Content, as ever, with a purpose in hand, Señor Lopez de Rego picked a few of the more useful of Hector's tools out of the debris, and strode off manfully towards the wall.

Caspar picked a little blue fragment of mosaic out of his lover's hair. What price their great historical heritage now? Señor Lopez de Rego hadn't even noticed it. Tory had gone off home. You could, of course, count on Gilly not to mind either way, if that caused less trouble. And from the look of sheer relief on Mrs Collett's face, she was glad to be rid of the whole sorry boiling. So much for the timeless and the priceless! It was, as usual, the poor old here and now, the flawed and vulnerable, that took possession of the living heart. Tenderly, he lifted William's chin, to see the state of him. Pale as a grub, and filthy from his battle with the garden. But not a sign of tears. Oh, God! Had his most precious William turned to stone? Would he forgive? In Caspar's ears rang Barbara's fond pronouncement: 'Caspar, I trust you always to know exactly what he needs.' Oh, dear, sweet Barbara! Had she been *wrong*?

Riddled with guilt, Caspar stepped back and waited for his sentence. Equally guilty, William stared back at him. He knew what Caspar was thinking. There would be floods of tears, and storms of rage, and nights of drunken nightmares. How had he borne with it through all the years? It must have been a vale of living hell. Was he a saint, like Barbara, to struggle on, and even take one last and desperate risk to extirpate the root of sickness at its very source, and heal his heart, the same way Barbara, if she had the power, would heal her damaged souls, and make them walk?

But Caspar was wrong. All that was over now. It was a different William who stood in front of him. From the beloved fingers, he prised the little blue fragment of mosaic and held it tight, like one of Barbara's precious beads, token of a new start. Caspar would come to see that, just as the world and his wife finally grow up, and leave their childhoods behind them, so had he. They'd drive together through the gates of Cold Domain, and, as usual, even before they reached the bypass, Caspar would forgive him.

The future, like the road, would lie ahead.

Discover more about our forthcoming books through Penguin's FREE newspaper...

Penguin
Quarterly

It's packed with:

- exciting features
- author interviews
- previews & reviews
- books from your favourite films & TV series
- exclusive competitions & much, much more...

READ MORE IN PENGUIN

In every corner of the world, on every subject under the sun, Penguin represents quality and variety – the very best in publishing today.

For complete information about books available from Penguin – including Puffins, Penguin Classics and Arkana – and how to order them, write to us at the appropriate address below. Please note that for copyright reasons the selection of books varies from country to country.

In the United Kingdom: Please write to *Dept. EP, Penguin Books Ltd, Bath Road, Harmondsworth, West Drayton, Middlesex UB7 0DA*

In the United States: Please write to *Consumer Sales, Penguin USA, P.O. Box 999, Dept. 17109, Bergenfield, New Jersey 07621-0120*. VISA and MasterCard holders call 1-800-253-6476 to order Penguin titles

In Canada: Please write to *Penguin Books Canada Ltd, 10 Alcorn Avenue, Suite 300, Toronto, Ontario M4V 3B2*

In Australia: Please write to *Penguin Books Australia Ltd, P.O. Box 257, Ringwood, Victoria 3134*

In New Zealand: Please write to *Penguin Books (NZ) Ltd, Private Bag 102902, North Shore Mail Centre, Auckland 10*

In India: Please write to *Penguin Books India Pvt Ltd, 706 Eros Apartments, 56 Nehru Place, New Delhi 110 019*

In the Netherlands: Please write to *Penguin Books Netherlands bv, Postbus 3507, NL-1001 AH Amsterdam*

In Germany: Please write to *Penguin Books Deutschland GmbH, Metzlerstrasse 26, 60594 Frankfurt am Main*

In Spain: Please write to *Penguin Books S. A., Bravo Murillo 19, 1° B, 28015 Madrid*

In Italy: Please write to *Penguin Italia s.r.l., Via Felice Casati 20, I-20124 Milano*

In France: Please write to *Penguin France S. A., 17 rue Lejeune, F-31000 Toulouse*

In Japan: Please write to *Penguin Books Japan, Ishikiribashi Building, 2-5-4, Suido, Bunkyo-ku, Tokyo 112*

In Greece: Please write to *Penguin Hellas Ltd, Dimocritou 3, GR-106 71 Athens*

In South Africa: Please write to *Longman Penguin Southern Africa (Pty) Ltd, Private Bag X08, Bertsham 2013*

BY THE SAME AUTHOR

Taking the Devil's Advice

'Staying the summer with his ex-wife, Oliver spends the warm days writing his autobiography in the laundry cupboard ... A pedant-philosopher, his head in the clouds of abstraction, he is continually stubbing his toes on domestic details and trampling over finer feelings ... literary efforts are continually interrupted by his scornful children while the manuscript is sabotaged by Constance's very different interpretation of the past ... Anne Fine's black comedy bounces along its sprightly one-liners without flagging' – *Observer*

'It is said to take two to make a quarrel but the *casus belli* for Constance after sixteen years of marriage is her philosopher husband Oliver's serene unawareness of ever having given grounds for one ... clever and entertaining ... a direly witty achievement' – *Guardian*

'Alive with brazen charm' – *Mail on Sunday*

BY THE SAME AUTHOR

The Killjoy

Nobody, not even his former wife Margaret, has ever treated Ian Laidlaw in a natural way. Presented with his hideous facial scars, everyone he meets reliably falls back on cast-iron, distant courtesy to hide pity or disgust or shock. But then Alicia Davie, a careless young student, breaks the rules totally by laughing in his face. Alicia goes on to infiltrate the hidden man, exposing the obsessive, destructive passions that lurk beneath his primly cordial manner, never realizing that she is playing with fire …

'Anne Fine's art makes us enter the fierce, logical predatory mind of the intelligent Beast as he corrodes within and exploits his willing victim … Haunting' – *The Times*

'Definitely not one for the faint-hearted. It's compellingly written, sinister … and very, *very* fine' – *Woman's World*